WAR OF
THE ANIMALS

Book 3: *The Crown of Crowns*

Jonathan DeCoteau

Animus Nor Books

waroftheanimals.com

Paperback ISBN: 979-8-9885704-4-8

eBook ISBN: 979-8-9885704-5-5

TABLE OF CONTENTS

For God and family

Other Books in Jonathan DeCoteau's War of the Animals *Series*

War of the Animals Book 1: The Shut Face of Thunder
A failed effort to weaponize animals awakens their intellects. The military responds by creating death camps to exterminate infected animals. Moon Shadow, an Arctic white wolf, unites with White Claw, a polar bear king, to form Animus, the first animal republic. Tensions between mankind and the animals escalate until Hunter General Brigand and Hunter Sgt. Fowler, human emissaries, recognize Animus as a country, disband the camps, and negotiate peace. The uneasy peace is broken with the rise of Azaz, lord of the grizzly bears. Azaz attacks human settlements, considering humans an invasive species that wreaks havoc on bears and the environment. Azaz forms his own death camps for humans. A world war breaks out as animals face humans and each other to see who will become the true apex species.

War of the Animals Book 2: Cry of the Gods
A generation after the events of The Shut Face of Thunder, Thraxis strikes. The anaconda queen resurrects long-dead species of dinosaurs to create an army that will allow her to rule the seven continents of Animus like her great ancestors, the dinosaurs, once did. Yet, Thraxis is not concerned only with power. The serpent queen issues a dire warning to the animal world: the animals must unite under her rule before the whale god King Blu attacks and kills them all. Just as the animals fight to overthrow Thraxis, the whale god breaches for the first time in thousands of years. Thraxis confronts the whale god, a creature so powerful that none have seen him and survived. War is inevitable.

Coming in 2024:

War of the Animals Book 4: Azaz, King of Kings
In the years after The Great Awakening, a young cub witnesses human hunters kill his mother. The cub attacks and kills his mother's murderers. Humans capture the surprisingly vicious cub, study and torture him. After a single act of mercy, the cub escapes. Vowing revenge on humankind, the grown bear leads the first assaults on humanity, defeating bear clan kings and humans alike until there is only one: Azaz, King of Kings..

PROLOGUE

Life and death are two winds that blow over the same sea, Snow Prophet scrawled on The Holy Tablets. *One speaks gently, the other harshly, but if you listen long enough, they become one and the same breeze. So it was in The Great War of the Sea, when gods became animals and animals became gods. The whispers of glory still haunt the winds for any animals that care to listen. Burn brightly, brothers and sisters, the whispers tell us, for every sun that rises shall one day burn no more, and every star that lights the night sky shall die in the light of a new day. This is the story of how death became life, and life, death, of how the suns and the stars came to burn in glory, and of how the winds of war became great, guiding winds of peace.*

CHAPTER 1

Pygopolis
The Canadian Ocean

In the beginning, there was only darkness. Black, briny waters that never seemed to know the sun's light. Volcanic clouds that lorded over the sky with sulfur and fire. Thunder that became the voice of the gods. Lightning that became the fingers of the divine, reaching down to spark the waters with new life.

Even the ancient whale god–at this point, the smallest of organisms–had no memory beyond the sensation of lightning striking water. Whether *Avrah* and King Blu existed before this, in a great void before the fire-scarred world trembled with new life, even the whale god cannot say for sure. Just that all that was, was indeed conscious. All was featureless, a single common life that gave birth to all. There was never a time when the smallest of microorganisms did not speak to one another, as they fused from bacteria in vents and became molecules and the molecules became life. There was never a time when the first algae-like plants took to the ocean waters that King Blu did not feel a part of All That Was. They were all *Avrah*, and *Avrah* was all, united with King Blu, the perfect harmony of a singular mind. And yet, the whale god, or that which became the divine whale, remembered even then the urge of *Avrah* to separate, to create more. And so, King Blu separated from *Avrah*, if only in spirit, and the two became mirror gods. The molecules combined in multifarious and wondrous ways, creating the first land plants that came. King Blu was among them, living ages as the first of the trees, before his essence transferred to the air and soil. King Blu spent eons traveling the winds of the earth until the ocean called him forth. King Blu became the corals, the jellyfish, the firmament of the sea, giving birth, in mad epiphany, to the creatures of the waters. In each eon, King Blu's physical form died. The whale's consciousness traveled farther, becoming *Pakicetus,* a land-roaming ancestor of the great gods of the sea. As the sun seasons blurred into one another, King Blu took to the sea again, becoming the prehistoric giant that lorded the waters for thousands of years.

As a young whale, King Blu was gentle, a holy vessel of *Avrah* celebrating all the life that the god spawned. Yet, as the divine masculine to *Avrah's* divine feminine, King Blu experienced the glory of physical life in a way that his second half did not. The pain of birth, and of death, never touched the purity of *Avrah*. She was a sky god who stood above. Yet, King Blu felt not just his death, but the birth and death of every creature of the sea that spawned from him, intensely, as if it were his own. The two gods kept creating, King Blu in the sea, and *Avrah* in the land. *Avrah* created the flying lizards and King Blu the sea lizards. Still, they felt the need to create more. It became a competition between the gods. When the great meteor of the heavens spiraled into the planet, they created still more creatures for the new earth and sea. King Blu created the earliest of fish, the octopus, the shark, and kept refining his masterpiece, the whale. King Blu saw the whale as the epitome of creation, an elegant creature that existed in complete harmony with its environment. And so, he bestowed it with god-like powers, such as the gift of intelligence and the gift of song. Yet, *Avrah*, not to be outdone, created her own masterpiece, a creature that walked on two legs who could handle the earth in its hands and praise *Avrah* in its songs. To King Blu, this was blasphemy, a standing apart from the world of nature and from the gods. The gods could not agree on which creature should rule and on who won their competition of life.

Let us be at peace, my brother, Avrah said after eons. *Clearly, I have won. Your whales stay the same, while my creatures grow and invent creatures of their own. They create all the time! They master the lands, the waters, and the air. They are my feet upon the world.*

Yet, my creatures have swum for endless sun cycles and are more in touch with the world of nature than yours are, King Blu responded, after still more eons. *The whales are gentle and noble and pure. They show the harmony of all life, joining with it, not seeking to arrogantly stand above their own god.*

We cannot agree who won, then, Avrah said. *Let the eons pass, and we shall see.*

Agreed, King Blu said. *And when I win, sister, will you agree to see the error of your ways? Will you let me erase your creatures so that you can start anew in creation?*

Only if you agree to let me do the same to your whales, Avrah said, *should I win.*

Eons passed, and the children of King Blu grew strong, as did the children of *Avrah*. The time of choosing finally came, the day one innocent whale, a sperm whale, sought to communicate with the children of *Avrah*. The whale sang its song of greeting, seeking to bridge the land that had divided *rulku* and whale for time immemorial, but there was no answer. The whale breached golden waters, dancing with the ocean to dazzle the children of *Avrah*. Still, there was no answer. And so, the whale and his brothers and sisters surrounded the great bark bodies of the sea, greeting the children of *Avrah* up close. It was then that the children of *Avrah*, the *rulku*, showed their true spirit. Instead of returning the whales' greeting in song, the *rulku* harpooned and speared the children of King Blu, killing them. The innocent children of King Blu, stricken and helpless, cried out to the gods for justice as their blood spilled all over the sea.

Avrah sought to inspire her children to find other ways to fuel their needs. Yet, King Blu saw the rivers of blood spill in the open ocean. He felt every wound, every whale cry, every death, from the tiniest calf to the greatest creature of the sea. When the children of *Avrah* had hunted the children of King Blu to near extinction, the whale god declared the challenge over.

No more of my children's blood shall go to your vicious killers, King Blu said. *Clearly, I was right. It is better for our creatures to be in harmony with nature than to try to shine and stand above, as gods do.*

Seeing the blood fill the waters, *Avrah* cried. *I am so sorry, divine twin,* Avrah said. *In my great pride, I have caused you and your children great pain. You were right. You have won. I cry and cannot be consoled. I finally know the pain you feel. Let your great wisdom determine the fate of my evil children. For each child that dies, I shall feel as you have, a pain beyond all imagining. In this, we shall be as one.*

I will pass judgment on the rulku, King Blu said. *But you will not cry forever, deified one. We shall create again. I will help you use the madness of the rulku and their machines to create new lords of the earth from the wonderful creatures you already created.*

And what if they also turn to evil, as the rulku have? Avrah asked.

Then the sea shall swallow them, and we shall start anew, King Blu said. *For no creature is above Avrah, and no creature is above King Blu.*

Pali-Ko

Deep South Pacific Ocean

Near the deepest waters where King Blu kept close to the beating heart of the earth, circled The Eyes of The God, as the great council was called. The lords of the sea swam in the sacred waters King Blu nourished with his preternatural wisdom and warmth. The majestic blue light of the divine was everywhere. Yet, none dared look too far into the waters, lest they see the maddening eyes of the whale god staring back at them. The whales, from the fabled blue whales to sperm whales to the mighty orcas, had a good many representatives. Wylaka, the great orca hunter, was among the wisest of the council. Xrata represented the military might of the great white sharks. Still, a host of other sharks, from the goblin shark to the Greenland shark, also had members that swam among the council and had less militant aims than their great white shark brethren. The dolphins made their opinions known, and Tee-Ha, their queen, was among the most vocal council members. Qylar the Hunter represented the giant octopi and provided intelligence updates. Also sifting through the deep currents were Krylakis, the greatest giant squid to emerge since his older brother, the Kraken, fell in The Serpent War. Not least among the influential council members was Jylar, the oldest giant clam in the ocean, with a brilliant pink-gray shell that defied even the mightiest of foes.

Beneath the council, in stirring currents of raw electricity, swam the monstrous King Blu, giving energy and life to the waters just as he took energy from them. A great electrical blue and gold aura formed around the massive creature, as if the primordial whale were an underwater sun. King Blu shone brilliantly, even in the deepest, farthest waters. His eyes were like blue stars coming down from the heavens, always with pupils that resembled the sphere of the Earth afire. And his head—still showing prehistoric touches, like the teeth of the *basilosaurus*—was a massive cranium that carried inside it the largest brain of any creature ever upon the earth. Hints of the full scope of the blue whale, and of the black and white stripes of the orca, still showed through the deeper waters. King Blu's colorings, even the blue and gold, were made up almost entirely of light. The whale god remained resting in his deep water den. King Blu shielded the council from full view of his godly eyes lest they go mad. Instead, he gave from his energy, strengthening his top admirals before the march to war.

"Sacred one," Qylar The Hunter said, without looking directly at his master. "The bickering of the council is futile. My octopi and crabs have labored many upwellings upon the generating sun Emperor Feng and his dragons assailed. We believe it is now fully operational and considerably more advanced. Your thoughts alone, my king, can command the waters, pillars or no pillars. At last, we can end this *landling* threat once and for all."

"No *landling* would have the power to destroy such a vast energy source," King Blu said. "I sense my sister, Avrah, helps the land animals still. She awakens, and so she awakens her animal fighters. What of the seven deadly plagues?"

"Lord and god," Xrata said, "for many sea seasons have my sharks toiled. The plague monsters are ready, precisely as you commanded. Surely, divine one, you know this, but releasing all the monsters will end life on this planet."

"Death is just new life not yet born," King Blu said. "I am The Maker and The Unmaker of Worlds. It is time that the *landlings* learn that I, not *Avrah*, am their true master, the sole jury and arbiter of their fate."

The whale god gathered his thoughts, closing his massive eyes. His aura swept the ocean, taking into view the full power of his oceanic might. Xrata had thousands of great white soldiers–the natural born that the *rulku* had not yet killed off with global warming, and the hybrids that commanded the great megalodon beasts, *cretoxyrhina,* and buzzsaw sharks resurrected by the dark magic of King Blu. Their sister sharks, from blacktip reef sharks and bull sharks to requiem sharks and tiger sharks, also readied their formations, many just as lethal, if not more so, than the great white sharks of record. The whale pods swam in force, led by Wylaka and the orcas near shore; the crafty mind of Sykla, the ancient sperm whale survivor of countless *rulku* whale boat attacks; and Sea Mountain, the greatest of the blue whales outside of the divine one himself. The whale forces numbered at least one million strong. The jellyfish, currently led by the lion's mane jellyfish Tempra, stayed to the flanks beside Krylakis's giant squid forces, thousands strong. Lastly, Qylar's special forces swam up to the front, from the giant octopus legions to Japanese spider crabs and coconut crabs, led by Jagged Claw, the most voracious hunter the crab world had ever known. Qylar would be in charge of the great plague monsters once the time was right.

"I sense the will of the waters. The time is at hand," King Blu said after much meditation. "*Ku-Rah* still cries for vengeance. Alert King Croc to lead the assault on *Yvot-Sing* to attack precisely where The Night Eye crows land. Tell him that The Army of The Black Ocean swims behind him."

"As you command, divine one," Xrata said.

"My lord," Tee-Ha said, swimming around the great den of the giant god. "What of the fatalities? Are all animals to suffer equally for the sins of their leaders?"

King Blu pondered the point. He answered, after deep contemplation, "The Dragon Lord will suffer the most for his infringement upon our kingdom. Any who have chosen his dominion have chosen death. Whales and sharks," King Blu commanded. "Once The First Plague Monster attacks, I will open the waters. Drag whatever lives to the ocean waters, kill it, and feast to your delight. Make sure Feng's subjects see only blood upon the waters."

"And what of Feng and The Dragon Guard?" Qylar The Hunter asked.

"I leave that to you and The Second Plague Monster," King Blu said. "Bring The Dragon Lord before me."

"And if he is too dangerous?" Qylar asked.

"Before this war is done, Feng shall look into the eyes of his god," King Blu said, "and enter my service. His fury and mine shall be as one. Release The First Plague Monster on *Yvot-Sing*. The madness of the animal world ends now. My judgment is proclaimed."

The whales bowed before their master, raising up a vicious war song. Sea Mountain sent the death song through the depths, while Wylaka took the song to the striking orcas in the front lines.

Awakened, The First Plague Monster stirred. The metallic monster made up of endless nanobots blasphemed the image of The Dragon Lord as it arose, flying alone towards the mainland. A giant dragon-like creature with one-hundred eyes all over its body and one-hundred black wings, The First Plague Monster became as fire, setting the sky ablaze with the tips of its razor wings.

CHAPTER 2

Rul-Seerus

Mount Asgard
Nunavut, Canada

Snow Prophet looked down from his perch upon the giant wolf statue that would welcome all animals to *Animus Nor.* In the many sun cycles since The Serpent War, the seas had grown restless. The waters ebbed and flowed as always, but there was a simmering beneath the surface, as if the waves were simply waiting for the opportune moment to taste animal blood. Yet, there were moments of divine grace. Moon Shadow's funeral, attended by all the animal lords, was one such turning of seasons. Animals knew that they no longer had their great mother to look after them, to outwit and outrun and outmaneuver whatever tyrant the madness of power brought next. And so, the animals all came up to the great wolf dens of the North, bowing their heads. Eagles, apes, elephants, bears, and dragons alike bowed in homage to the wolf who lost her own cubs, only to become a mother to the world. And in the whispers of the wind, they heard some of the wisdom of Moon Shadow: reckless hunts had no place in the animal world. Only animal brotherhood and sisterhood would end the madness of war.

The majestic snowy owl admired the care the head wolf artist, Cave Sun, showed in creating the might of the bones and paws, the majesty of the mane. Yet, the eyes were like the eyes of many temple gods, full of distant might, but empty of the beating heart that drove the wolf queen to greatness. The owl oracle marveled that he had lived long enough to see a simple arctic wolf, abducted by the *rulku,* rise to the status of a god. Yet, Snow Prophet knew, even then, that such an apotheosis was necessary. The wolves needed a unifying belief, something to unite them in the times of rising darkness. And Moon Shadow shimmered as all that was bright in a dark and sometimes moonless night. Of all the ancestor gods the animals came to worship, none seemed more deserving of the honor.

Unbeknownst to the prophet, Sky Death flew just behind him, perching atop *Rul-Seerus*.

"It almost makes you feel like she's still here with us," Sky Death said. "Doesn't it, old friend?"

"So few of us are left now," Snow Prophet said. "Yet, I endure one flap of the wings at a time."

"My skin grows tight on my bones," Sky Death said. "It's a most ironic look for a bird of prey."

"You look well, my old friend," Snow Prophet said.

"Can it be that a seer lies?" Sky Death said with a cackle. "Perhaps these old eyes have seen it all."

"Not all of it, no," Snow Prophet said, mulling over the last words as he spoke them. "I fear more of us may soon join with *Avrah*. Pale Ghost trains his great-grandchildren to take his place. It is said no mouse has ever lived as long as the one touched by the evil magic of the *rulku*. Zulta is sick and may pass at any moment now. Even Thunder Killer is an old king now, readying his son to take his throne. All of those who remember the world of the *rulku* will soon pass, lost to legend."

"Except for you, wise owl," Sky Death said. "Something tells me that you will live forever."

"Only legends live forever," Snow Prophet said. "So I said of Moon Shadow once. All of this, all that we've fought for, will one day be little more than words some talon scrawls on a slate. But who shall read that slate? Who shall learn from those words?"

At that moment, Cave Sun approached, a lanky gray wolf whose bony body suggested a total, if unnecessary, sacrifice for the arts. The artist wolf arched his head, staring at the statue. Cave Sun asked, "Something seems a bit off, perhaps in the eyes. I feel that they are missing something, a wayward spark that I can't quite kindle."

"Hope," Snow Prophet said. "Moon Shadow's eyes were always full of hope."

Cave Sun turned back, commanding his ape apprentices to chip away at the eyes a bit more.

"I remember when I first saw her, a determined arctic wolf answering the call that burned in her blood. It led her north, to me," Sky Death said. "I never thought the day I ran into a pushy, half-starved wolf would be one of the happiest day of my life."

"Meeting Moon Shadow was the happiest day of a great many lives," Snow Prophet said. "When you finish with the great wolf, will there be more to the sculpture?" he asked.

Cave Sun turned, shaking his head and saying, "We wanted Moon Shadow to stand alone, above all land animals, greeting them as they entered the first land of animalkind."

"Moon Shadow never stood alone," Snow Prophet replied. "You should include her pups. And you should include different species of animals behind them. She was a mother to us all."

Cave Sun chatted with the apes, considering the matter.

Just then, a hawk, battle-scarred, with savage eyes, flew overhead. The hawk shrieked for all to hear, calling out the name of Thunder Killer in corrupted avian *Osine*.

"Land here, gentle bird," Sky Death said. "King Thunder Killer is many sun cycles away, in the land of the setting sun."

The hawk coughed up blood, collecting itself from its extraordinary flight.

"How long have you been flying?" Sky Death asked.

"An Amur falcon, from the land of the dragon, met me a little ways over the open waters," the hawk said. "My name is Orij. I had to fight crows to deliver this message. I never saw so many crows swarm at once. They nearly took out my eyes and my feathers, but a hawk's claws are not to be toyed with. They gave me my life this very day. I live to tell you that The War of The Whale God is upon the land of the dragon. King Blu has awoken! The dread god sends a plague upon the animals of *Yvot-Sing*. Many animals die. The waves grow large as the dragon prepares his border for a great ocean offensive strike. The whale god blocks the nanosphere. Yet, Feng cries out for allies."

Snow Prophet and Sky Death looked at one another.

"What shall I tell the Amur falcon?" Orij asked, still recovering her breath.

"Orij, you have given your life to get here. That is enough to give," Snow Prophet said. "I will fly and give our reply when the time is right. First, we must meet with the animal lords and alert the animal world as to what transpires. If King Blu means to avenge himself upon Feng, he means to avenge himself upon us all. For now, eat and rest."

"There is no time for meetings," Orij said. "If the dragons fall, what defense will we have against the whale god?"

"Be calm," Snow Prophet said, closing his eyes. "We know of one who can read the thoughts of the whale god. We will answer this attack, but this is only the beginning. Rest, Orij. Take one last taste of peace. It may be your last taste for quite some time."

Orij flapped the water from her wings and let her eyes shut.

"Get Pale Ghost and his great-grandchildren," Snow Prophet said to Sky Death.

"The blind mouse?" Sky Death asked. "Can we expect him to be of service after so many moons?"

"The blind may be leading the blind," Snow Prophet said, "but if anyone has a chance of getting a message to the animal lords, it's Pale Ghost."

Sky Death flew off, leaving Snow Prophet to look after the emerging statue of the wolf queen. Her eyes, whiter in the open sun, had the faintest glimmer of hope in them.

"Look after us now," Snow Prophet said to the burgeoning statue. "We need all the hope your soul can give, mother wolf."

CHAPTER 3

Yvot-Sing
Beijing, China

Alazar The Red shrieked fire, sounding the great alarm. The red-crowned cranes, white-naped cranes, and Chinese sparrowhawks did the same. Fyvol, exalted captain of The Dragon Guard, circled the tempests twice. The wily dragon commander made sure that the raging typhoon of cloud and lightning could be out-flown. Thereafter, The Dragon Guard flew throughout the temple city of *Yvot-Sing*, sending up the alarm to the giant pandas, leopards, spider monkeys, and snakes still swarming the animal city pathways. The great, red wings of Alazar became like a beacon as he followed after his captain, shrieking in crude *Osine* for all animals to seek immediate shelter.

Ty-Ry, the elder giant panda, gathered the running animals with his white-black paws. They ran towards the sanctuary of the mighty dragon temple, saying prayers to Yu The Golden Nightmare, The Ascended Panda. Even The Rat King emerged from his hole, leading burrowing animals like the pangolins to firmer shelter under the magnificent monuments of the dragon.

Emperor Feng, Scourge of the Southern Seas, rose from his great throne lair, his wings eclipsing the clouds. Feng watched as the great winds swallowed up grebes and white-bellied sea eagles, consuming the sky.

"Dragon Guard," Feng ordered. "Gather around me. We shall dispel this threat with a fire ring."

"My king, won't the trapped animals fall?" Fyvol asked.

Feng answered, "Our first duty is to the city. Those animals have tasted death already."

The dragons circled around their ferocious leader. The son of Thraxis opened his white jaws, releasing a golden fire into the air. Fyvol, Alazar and the other dragon masters, from Palavir The Black to Thrysta The Green, released their fire, joining with the magic of their master. The great fire wall in the sky consumed any moisture that neared it. Some animals fell into flames. Others flew to freedom. A few looked at the great fire shield forming around the city as the dragons extended along all sides.

"My king," Ty-Ry called, running as best he could along the ground. "The obelisks!"

Feng turned to see the crushed residue of the discarded stone. Long ago, his dragons had made short work of the portals of the whale god. Yet, the stones flew from the ground, some from the fire, coalescing once more not into a portal so much as into a sign of flame.

"The storms are the breath of the whale god," Fyvol told the king. "Wherever they are, the whale god and his Army of the Black Ocean are not far behind."

"We must move the enchanted stone from the city," Feng said. "Quick. Burn it to ashes."

The dragons formed around the stone. A great white dancing flame, like a star caught by the fire of the rising sun, set upon the great stone. No matter how much the great dragons blew, the stone only abSurbed the fire, growing more radiant.

"Truly, this is the work of a god," Palavir said.

"Dragon Guard," Feng said, "lift the stone. We have no time!"

The dragons flew with their massive weight against the stone. Still, the pillar did not budge. Feng flew with his massive legs striking at the stone. Only then did it tilt enough for the dragons to lift the puzzling mystery of stone and fire. The great stone seemed to fight back, growing heavier as it reached down to the earth. Feng flew around with all of his power and thrusted the stone past the fire ring.

Only then did the dragon emperor see the storm winds take shape. Beyond the shield of smoke and flame, black nanobots swarmed. They coalesced into thousands of eyes and wings, taking the body of a great silver-black dragon, easily twice the size of the dragon emperor himself. The giant dragon roared, spewing nanobots of fire over the lands and winds of *Yvot-Sing*. Only the durability of dragon fire kept the massive creature from the heart of the crown city.

The plague monster and Feng locked eyes. In the pupils of the monster, Feng saw a cyclone of water and wind emanating from the portal, pouring over dry land. A small sea formed. With it, an entire legion of orcas, led by a wily brute of black and white markings, Wylaka. Interspersed were the shark legions, with blacktip reef sharks and bull sharks leading the charge. The great white sharks, with megalodon troops among the number, formed a perimeter. Feng turned to look at the assaulting animals. He saw their admiral, and King Blu's champion, the monstrous, mangled great white leader, Xrata, ordering the sharks from afar. Spider monkeys, Siberian weasels, and wild boars shrieked. The nascent sea washed over their noses and snouts. A great roar, like thunder twice removed, swept the waters. Then, all was silent as the lifeless bodies sank into the new sea. The ocean was everywhere, and so was death. Xrata arched his back, signaling his sharks. Wylaka let out a whistle to his orcas. The sea predators swooped in. The only relief the dragon emperor felt was that the gentle creatures under his rule could not feel the unrelenting jaws of megalodon and great whites taking giant chunks of flesh from their bones.

"What now, my emperor?" Fyvol asked. "Do we just protect those inside the wall?"

Feng thought for a moment. "You must not let the forces of the whale god through the dragon fire," he said, "whatever the cost. I will deal with this monster."

"Two of us will go with you, my lord," Thrysta The Black said. "Three of us will stay here."

"Stay above the waters," Feng said. "We must take out the dragon first."

The Plague Dragon reared up, seeing the three dragon lords flying straight for its cyclone body.

"I am Judgment," the beast said, simply.

"And I am Insolence," Feng replied. "I send your petty god a message: King Blu will burn for what he has done!"

The Dragon Guard flanked their great dragon emperor, flying into the dragon's heart. Feng opened his massive jaws, releasing liquid fire along the nanobots comprising the dragon's vital organs. The nanobots, in vast swaths of skin and scales, dropped to the ocean. The Plague Dragon laughed and reassembled, every bit as massive as before.

"Death waits for no one," The Plague Monster said. "Even emperors fall to herald of King Blu."

Nanobots swarmed to the earth below, replicating in buzzing hives of activity. The parasitic nanobots attached to the bodies of the few South China tigers that swam, fending off the sharks. The tiger eyes became black as the South China tigers took their last breaths, becoming little more than fresh pools of blood upon an already sanguine sea.

Feng roared. His throat glowed bright gold with the dragon fire he called from the heart of his being. The Dragon Guard did as their master did, conjuring up ungodly fires.

"Even gods fall," Feng said.

In a wave of golden-red light, the flames combined, scorching what was left of The Plague Dragon. Its massive metallic body writhed, becoming a fire of liquid gold. The fire glistened in the reflected sea light before The Plague Dragon, only embers and ash, plunged into the sea.

Xrata looked up at the beasts that slayed The Plague Dragon.

"Plunge into the waters," Feng said. "Kill every shark or whale that doesn't flee."

Unleashing a plume of flame that could boil even the ocean waters, The Dragon Guard descended. The steam-ridden smoke from the contact of water and flame became a camouflage for the great dragon beasts. The bull sharks and black tip reef sharks swarmed. Alazar and Thrysta grasped the sharks with their claws, impaling them. The dragons tore the sharks in half, depositing their bloody carcasses so as to further obscure the waters. Suddenly, Feng plunged into the waters, taking up two great white sharks and impaling them. In retaliation, Xrata nodded his massive head. The megalodons emerged, biting at the dragons with jaws of primordial power. The dragons ascended from the flaming waters, the fires dancing upon their wings. Three megalodons breached with their great jaws, hungry and open, ready to strike. Feng blew fire down upon the prehistoric monsters' throats until the sharks' bodies burned from the inside out. Wylaka led a pod of killer whales, who nipped at the dragons. Alazar The Red lifted a killer whale from the waters and the other dragons set it aflame.

With an arch of his spine, Xrata sent orders to his sharks. Wylaka clicked and whistled at his whale legions. The sharks pulled back, as did the killer whales.

Just when the exhausted dragon emperor thought victory was assured, Feng saw the reason for Xrata's move. King Croc, with an entire battalion of gigantic prehistoric *imperators*, was sailing in a massive ship of *rulku* design. Lasers, not unlike dragon fire, rained upon the fire shield. Even The Dragon Guard was not immune. A few laser blasts struck Thrysta, who roared in agony.

"What now, my lord?" Alazar The Red asked.

"There are too many of them," Feng said. "Fly back while I hold off King Croc. Summon the animal lords. Request assistance. Tell them how dire the situation in *Yvot-Sing* is. But also tell them that we spared their kingdoms The First Plague."

"I will not leave you alone, my lord," Alazar said.

Feng whipped his head around, commanding: "Go now, or all hope is lost. The Dragon Guard and I will unseat the crocodile king–in time."

Alazar bowed and flew off. Feng assisted Thrysta in flying back through the fire shield. There, the remaining Dragon Guard circled and watched, calculating.

Gangra Dytche

Nunavut, Canada

The Polar Regions

Thunder Killer still had strength in his white-tipped brown wings, which had a remarkable spread for a bird so battle-tested and so ancient and wise. His son, Pale Thunder, flew close at his side, as did Sunfire and Blood Talon, tried-and-true veterans of The Serpent War. Sky Death saw some of the father in the son, particularly in the strength of the wings and in the silent conviction of the eagle. Yet, there was a solemnity to the eagles' greeting, as if this was a last gathering of old friends before time and the elements made such gatherings impossible. Pale Ghost and his great-grandchildren, the twins Silent Wind and Shadow Dancer, were among the assembly, crawling off the back of the hawks and the eagles, a sight that still astonished Sky Death to no end.

"Such strange winds have blown since those that first carried *rulku* magic," Sky Death said. "To think, the end would come like this, as a gathering of old warriors. I can think of no birds and mice I'd rather face the end with than all of you."

"Your compliment is much appreciated," Thunder Killer said. His voice was hoarse with age, but still had the same elegant nobility of years gone by. "But I don't intend for this to be the end. We've said goodbye to too many friends already, wise old bird."

"Agreed," Snow Prophet said, standing by Sky Death. "A friend is too rare a gift these days not to fight for."

The birds bowed their beaks and raised their wings in greeting to one another.

"So where are the other animal lords?" Thunder Killer asked.

"Still hunkered down, as the wise wolf suggested before The Fire Wolf came for her," Snow Prophet answered. "We have a noble bird, Orij, a hawk, who is here to present her request from the dragon emperor, or rather, his emissary, a brave Amur falcon who awaits a response. Feng cannot attend, needless to say. But if you gaze upon this loose approximation of the holosphere that once was, patched together by Pale Ghost's great-grandchildren, you can still see some of the old faces."

The birds and mice turned to view the holographic bodies of Dryga The Dignified, king of all bears, and Dasu, his old mountain leopard mentor. They lay in The Throne of Azaz, a great mountain cave, surrounded by attendant elks, pika, and moose. Ice Giant, considerably older and leaner than in moons past, also sat by the great bear king. In the same holographic spread were Klang Kru-gal and Yanta, the ruling powers of the jungle nations. Both looked very much the same, except for a serene light in the eyes of the ape king whose temples to Zehrah and Avrah were among the most elegant in the world. A new lion lord, Sun Stalker, Vyrillya's son, ruler of the big cats, lay among them. A new wolf queen-heir apparent, Moon Herald, a giant gray timber wolf, sat among the lands of the eagle. From the old lands of *Seerus-Ungalore* stood the image of Fire Hoof, the mystical reindeer with golden antlers who ruled after the fall of The Night Eye and Groth The Impaler. From *Animus Sur*, the great boa constrictor Xyla ruled, continuing the legacy of Thraxis The Conqueror. Near her was Ruth The Lawless, a *rulku* who had the look of ice on granite in her eyes. Methuse-lah and her sisters listened in, and lastly, Lady Diurnia, Methuselah's daughter, stood watching from *Drygopola,* in the land of the former *Rulkura.*

"Welcome, great animal lords," Snow Prophet said. "I bring with me Orij, the rough-legged hawk, who has a message of supreme importance."

Orij flew before the council, ragged and thin after so many suns of open flight. The ominous bird had black feathers at the bend of its wings and upon its fearsome bosom. White plumage graced the rest of its great wings. Its eyes were those of a true hawk: savage, wild, full of death.

"My fellow animals," Orij began. "The great dragon emperor lies besieged on all sides by the armies of the ocean. The great Amur falcon, Steel Wings, has flown many swathes of ocean and mountain to tell us of the threat. King Blu means to strike at all our lands once the great defender, Feng, Scourge of the Southern Seas, falls. King Blu means to raze all of *Yvot-Sing* to make an exam-ple for the other animal lords. Emperor Feng asks that the animal lords lend their troops to this battle, in return for the undying protection of The Dragon Guard in the battles ahead. My liege presents this," Orij began, tossing giant dead nanobots from his beak. "It is The First Plague monster, a hideous dragon, slain for all animals."

"Impressive," Xyla said. "Yet, only one plague has yet emerged. Who knows what else the whale god has in store for the dragon emperor and for us? We should tread carefully lest the plagues consume us before we can even strike."

"The serpent's mind and my mind are as one," King Dryga—older, with some white splotches among the reddish-brown fur—decreed. "The whale god must be fiercer than ever if the king of dragons begs help from us," he added. "Our first allegiance is to our own lands. The wily whale means to trick us. With all of us on an unproven field of battle, King Blu can rid the lands of their animal lords in one lethal strike."

"I never expected the great bear king to back down so willingly from a fight," Yanta interjected. "But these are strange tidings and even stranger days. I respectfully disagree with Queen Xyla and King Dryga. Animal lords must stand together or the whale god has already won. The dragon emperor played a crucial role in our victory in The Serpent War. His dragons bought us the time to build our forces. I say we do what we planned to do: strike and strike hard, with unremitting fury. But we shall not strike with animal forces. We shall strike as the whale god strikes–with cunning, with nanotechnology."

"A plague for a plague," Pale Ghost said, turning the matter over in his ingenious mouse cranium. "Sadly, that has become the animal way."

"We have the nanobots at our feet, thanks to Orij," Klang Krugal said. "Could we not find a way to turn the very plague back to the ocean that bred it?"

"Tread carefully," Sky Death said. "The ocean is the womb of all life on this planet. Poison the womb and you kill not only the mother but also the child."

A rattling hiss, half madness, half ecstasy, rose higher than even the growling voices of the most venerable animal lords. Sky Death, Snow Prophet and Pale Ghost turned to see the creature slithering forth, The Queen Of The Broken Crown, Thraxis The Terrible. Thraxis looked leaner than ever a snake had, her stomach digesting the rapturous fury of the whale god, so much so that she barely ate enough to keep alive. Thraxis' eyes were white as snow upon first frost. Her skin was its old green, bristling with electricity, as if she were a creature the whale god started to craft from clay but had just as quickly forgotten. Even in her slithering forth, Thraxis was writhing, as if even being contained in her body was a pain beyond compare.

All eyes joined those of Sky Death, Snow Prophet and Pale Ghost, astonished to see so mighty an empress fallen so low. Yet, even through their wonder, the animal lords sensed a certain manic mystic aura all around the great anaconda, as if the great snake empress were caught between two skins, one of this world, one of the world yet to come.

"Should Thraxis be so near the council?" King Dryga asked. "Is the snake queen not possessed by the spirit of King Blu?"

"Beware how you greet Death," Thraxis said, before anyone could restrain her. Her voice rose to the great heights of a hiss, only to plummet again. "Death is a keen judge of character. And Death's eyes, they are always watching. The whale god will judge you for your actions and any who fall short of his judgment will swim in the bloody abyss of the fallen ocean."

"She speaks gibberish," Sun Stalker said. "Remove her."

"No," Klang Krugal said. "Madness may be the mother of her words, but their father is wisdom."

"Klang Krugal speaks true," Snow Prophet said. "Let the nanobots that blind the snake witch's eyes share their vision."

Thraxis projected a small image of the whale god's larger plan. A new ocean was to be born in the land of *Yvot-Sing*. It would be unlike any ocean that existed before–fully, keenly alive. This ocean would be a mother and a predator. It would be a single organism, one powerful enough to entrap the mother spirit of *Avrah* herself. It would grow to be the world ocean, swallowing up lands as remote as *Ku-Rah* and as north as *Animus Nor*. And it would never stop growing until it swallowed the world, even itself, in a complete darkness not seen since before the world was born.

Thraxis' nanobots ceased transmitting their picture of doom. The fallen empress' body writhed again, as if the whale god, Death itself, were wrestling with her, yet unable to completely win.

The animals sat in stunned silence.

"This is worse than even I imagined," King Dryga said, if only to break the silence that preyed upon them. "If we attack as one, King Blu will kill us before we can come to our full power. If we do nothing, our most powerful animal lord falls. Truly, the whale god has the mind of a warrior."

"King Blu means to humble us," Sky Death said.

"I am humbled," Yanta said, "so I suppose his strategy worked."

Snow Prophet nodded. Dasu and her cougars dragged the unconscious fallen snake queen out of the assembly.

"To be broken does not mean being beaten," Snow Prophet said, upon Thraxis' departure. "The whale god has inadvertently shown us the path to victory."

"Did we watch the same vision?" Pale Ghost asked. "What victory can be had against such an awesome power as this?"

"*Avrah*," Snow Prophet said. "The way to beat the whale god is through *Avrah*."

"Are you on speaking terms with the mother of all creation?" Klang Krugal asked. "I've seen the eyes of *Avrah* in Zehrah, her prophet, before the dragon burned the holy one into the ashes of a firebird. None have seen him since–or her. The prophet is silent and so, it seems, is *Avrah*."

"*Avrah* is around us always," Snow Prophet said. "But we must remember her in our hearts. We must face King Blu and save as many lives as we can. But some of us, the holiest among us, must fly in search of The Firebird, the prophet of *Avrah*. Only *Avrah* has the power to bestow the status of a god upon us. And only then will King Blu fall."

"You sound just as mad as the snake queen," Sun Stalker said.

"Madness may be our only chance," Thunder Killer said. "But how can we find a bird that has burned himself into the sky, gone these many years?"

Snow Prophet looked directly into the uncertain yellow eyes of the gray and white-furred timber wolf Moon Herald.

"This is beyond my visions. We must commune with Moon Shadow–through you," Snow Prophet said. "We have the perfect place–her magnificent sculpture, near where she fell. We must have you channel your inner goddess and call your ancestor back, just as King Dryga did Azaz. Only then can we find The Firebird and end this war once and for all."

Moon Herald gulped, but she kept her eyes on those of the snowy owl prophet. "I accept," he said.

"If we reach Moon Shadow, and we find where The Firebird flies, Criddock and I will accompany you," Snow Prophet said, "to help you in any way you can."

"And the rest of us?" King Dryga asked.

Snow Prophet sighed. Looking each animal lord in the eyes, he said, "Your forces shall portal through, with the help of Pale Ghost's great-great grand-children, and send troops to face the whale god. Meanwhile, you shall ready yourselves, bolstering your remaining forces in your own countries. *Yvot-Sing* is just the beginning."

"Orij," Sky Death said. "I'm sure Steel Wings is ready to fly with the news that help is on the way."

"Very good, my lords," Orij said, flapping her wings, preparing for flight.

The animal lords watched Orij fly off. Snow Prophet turned to Empress Xyla.

"The prehistoric navy Thraxis The Conqueror put together," Snow Prophet said. "Is it ready?"

"It is," Xyla said, "though I shall need some beasts for my own lands."

"Of course," Snow Prophet said. "Show Pale Ghost where they are. You strike first, if you're up for it, great snake queen."

"Portals alone will not be enough," Empress Xyla said.

"I will operate any hovercraft still operational," Ruth the Lawless said.

Ruth now had the face of the crone, the heart of the mother, and the will of the maiden. Yet, Ruth was strong in her age, and her eyes showed her tenacity.

"Feng saved us all," Ruth said. "The least we can do is save him."

Snow Prophet's eyes looked off to the horizon. The eyes of the other animal lords followed his.

"What is it, oracle?" Sky Death asked.

"I am powerful, but to pull this off, we will need a witch of greater power still, and Thraxis is out of her mind," Snow Prophet said. "What of Methuselah?'

"Still recovering," Lady Diurnia said.

"Where, King Dryga, is your mother?" Snow Prophet asked.

King Dryga growled. "In exile," he said.

"Then we must make it to her before King Blu does," Snow Prophet said. "Send Ice Giant, bear king, to tell her what has happened here. The rest of us must prepare to go our separate ways until war once more joins us."

As Snow Prophet spoke the words, the ancient giant tortoise emerged. Criddock The Cudgel still bore pink, green and beige upon his mighty shell, along with red from the blood of the sea. Yet, he had the same question as always.

"Did I miss anything? Hopefully so," Criddock said. "These meetings are always so grim. It takes me seven full sun cycles to recover from one."

"It's not like you've ever been on time for one," Snow Prophet said. "I wonder how many sun cycles it would take you to recover from a full meeting."

"More suns than I have left," Criddock said. "What, in short, is the plan?"

"Madness," Snow Prophet said. "The plan is madness."

"You should have told me we had the same plan we always have *before* I made such a long trip," Criddock said with a moan. "It was a journey full of near misses with all kinds of sharks and jellyfish. *Avrah* be told, I hate jellyfish. I've never met one that I liked, unless it was my dinner."

Snow Prophet bid the animal lords farewell and nodded for Pale Ghost and Silent Wind to end the transmission.

As they did, Thraxis, from a far patch of ice, cackled. Snow Prophet looked towards the great snake, wondering if the same fate awaited all oracles bold enough to face King Blu.

CHAPTER 4

Dyr Vespa

Andes Mountains, South America

On the edge of a mountain peak, Aeyra sat, channeling the winds in front of him. Tradition long held that the winds carried the voices of the ancestors, and that if a *rulku* looked long enough, the spirits of their ancestors might appear in those winds. But for Aeyra, growing up without a father, sharing his mother with whatever *rulku* band needed protection from poachers, the winds felt silent. Yet, there was something that burned with the morning sun, a certainty that pained his skin more than the heat of the new day. Aeyra knew he was meant for something more. His meeting with the whale god had convinced him of that. There were thoughts in his head that were not his own, thoughts from the whale god that predated Creation. For lack of a better term, Aeyra could feel *Avrah* somewhere inside him, violently, like a wind coursing against his skin.

"Son," Ruth called. She used the term uneasily.

Whoever or whatever this boy once was, the snake empress had changed him. Aeyra grew stronger, older; he grew into a young man, but he grew alone.

"You're leaving again," Aeyra said, simply. "Off to another war."

"Our ability to navigate the thinking machines is all that keeps us alive," Ruth said, shaking the long black strands of her gnarled hair. "If only life weren't such a struggle, but it is."

"It's time for me to leave too," Aeyra said.

"But I need you here, looking after the sick and wounded," Ruth implored.

Aeyra laughed. "As if they'd let me near them," he said. "You see the same fear in their eyes whenever I'm around. I am not them, Mother, however much I wish I could be. I am something else entirely. I feel the night flowing through my veins. A terrible destiny calls me, one that shall devour me whole."

"You mustn't speak like that," Ruth said, touching Aeyra's shoulder. "You're your father's son."

"That's just it—I'm not," Aeyra said. "That's why I need to leave. I need to find my own way. I must find this destiny and wrestle it to the ground."

"The snake queen poisoned your mind," Ruth said. "You must stay and heal."

"Thraxis is a mother to me too, as hard as it may be for you to hear," Aeyra said. "I must see her again. I must talk to the oracles. I must set out."

"When I return," Ruth said. "Can't you find any peace, even in the winds?"

Aeyra shook his head. "I have no ancestors," he said. "Who is there to call me? I am alone."

Ruth kissed the top of her son's head. "In time," she said, "we will sort this all out. You will take my place as the new arch elder–but after you rest…and heal."

Aeyra looked back. He felt distant, cold, and warm all at the same time. "I will stay until the last child we rescued from the poachers heals. After that, I will leave. I'm trying to say goodbye to you, Mother, and to thank you for what you tried to do for me. When you come home, I won't be here. I tried coming home, Mother. For your sake, I tried to be the son you wanted. But sometimes, there is no coming home. I must find my way, as you found yours."

Ruth took her son's hand. "Go to Methuselah first," she said. "When Nurv-lyn walked among us, before he became The Firebird, he sought her council. If anyone knows your path, it's her." Ruth embraced her son. "I'm sorry it took us so long to rescue you. I'm sorry I wasn't a better mother."

"You were a great mother to all of your people," Aeyra said. "Now, it's time for me to look Destiny in the eye, whatever that destiny may be. But first, this magic within me, it must find its way out, into the world. The pain is too great."

"Methuselah can help you with that," Ruth said, taking out a small map. "This is where she was last seen, during The Serpent War. The animal world will protect her and test you, as will the trees. But if there is anyone that can help you, it's her."

Aeyra returned his mother's embrace. The stiffness of his embrace showed his indifference, but his eyes showed that he wished this were not so.

"Goodbye, Mother," he said simply. "May *Avrah* guide you in the fight ahead."

"And may you find peace," Ruth said, kissing Aeyra once more. "You'll always be my only son."

With that, Ruth rose, checking in among the people, making sure that the sick received the healing they needed.

Yvot-Sing

Beijing, China

Through the horizon, Alazar The Red spotted a mangled gray-plumed falcon fighting with a murder of crows. The falcon gouged with its talons, striking with its beak. The crows spouted incantations, poisoning the black eyes of the mighty messenger. Alazar The Red breathed fire, sending the crows off. The spies of The Night Eye disappeared, back to the shadows of pale-lit flame. Steel Wings flew forth, muttering with his last breaths.

"Tell the emperor help is on the way," Steel Wings said. "The animal lords prepare to protect their own kingdoms," the falcon said between breaths. "However, they send Thraxis' navy of pre-*rulku* beasts to match The Army of The Black Ocean. Take me to the emperor with all haste. I will tell him what the noble hawk Orij told me of the plans of the animal lords."

"Feng does all he can to hold off the assaults of King Blu," Alazar The Red said. "I've been sent to round up all able animals to face the threat of the sea."

"My news may well be the only sun he sees," Steel Wings said. "Please. I don't have much time."

Alazar The Red looked down at the fearless falcon, battered by wind and rain, at times just barely keeping its wings from the clutches of the rising sea mists. Here was an animal worthy of honor. Even the heart of the dragon could not help but feel pity.

"Very well," Alazar The Red said. "The only animals I see near the assaulting waters are dead ones, anyway. Come. Let me carry you. You've earned a rest, noble falcon."

The falcon accepted the perch of a dragon's paw. Steel Wings flinched slightly when the mighty dragon talons wrapped around his body. Yet, the unrelenting falcon knew that he could be in no safer place against the fury of the volatile tides. The dragon flew with almost preternatural speed. Entire cloud banks fell to the ocean after being sliced through by the mighty red wings. Yet, even Steel Wings cringed when he saw what the dragon flew towards. Feng and The Dragon Guard fought to stop the megalodons and crafty whales from finding a way to unleash the ocean waters in the throne city. It seemed like a hopeless task, like ancient *rulku* fighting to control the sea. Yet, Steel Wings knew that he carried hope upon his wings. The sooner the great dragon emperor learned that he had only to bide time, the better.

"Emperor Dragon," Steel Wings said as they came closer. "I have news from the animal lords."

"Fortify the dragon fire," Feng said to Alazar The Red. "Come with me to the throne city," he ordered Steel Wings.

"My lord," Alazar The Red said. "This noble falcon has flown the length of the great ocean. He is too weak to make the flight unaided."

"Then you will have my wings," Feng said, "and I will have your words."

Feng gently took the noble falcon within his talons, still red with shark blood. They flew away from The Dragon Guard, towards the towers of stone and bone that signaled the holy city. Many of the dragon's enemies' bones ended up there, from those of unfaithful servant snakes to those of crocodile spies evidently not very good at subterfuge. The dragon emperor flew to the highest perch, away from the range of any creeping lizard or flying spy. He placed the Amur falcon on the perch near him. The horizon glowed in dragon fire, a delicate gold and red balance. The air smelled of boiling blood.

"Are the lords coming, or are the dragons on their own?" Feng asked.

Steel Wings, a normally unflappable bird, looked up at the sheer size of the dragon before him. It was evident to all who looked upon Feng that he was truly meant as Thraxis' weapon of weapons in The Serpent War.

"Snow Prophet predicts that King Blu will be attacking their shores within a moon cycle," Steel Wings said. "The animal lords will oversee the protection of their own lands. However, they work to form a common army, an army of the sea to rival that of the whale god. This is the army they are sending to you, with prehistoric beasts of Thraxis' own design. It includes prehistoric sharks, whales, eels, and monstrous *leedsichthys,* giant squid, and megalodon to match the monsters of the deep."

"The animal lords grow scared," Feng said. "So much for old alliances. Yet, I will gladly accept their army of the sea, even if it only delays the inevitable. The armies of the ocean are simply too vast to overcome. We must find a way to make our lands like mine, rings of fire inhospitable to the waves of the deep."

"I still have might in my wings," Steel Wings said. "I can still fly back and tell the animal lords this message."

"No, Steel Wings," Feng said, with surprising gentility. "You have given enough. Perch here and find what rest you may before rest is found no more. I must fly off and tell The Dragon Guard the news."

Feng flew off, leaving the little falcon to gaze peacefully from the greatest perch of the land. Steel Wings saw the dragon emperor fly and roar to the dragons, who renewed the fire they rained down upon the megalodon beasts, turning them from massive sharks into flame-eaten black skeletons. Moments later, the first of Thraxis' sea army portaled through. Giant mechanical toothed whales, *leedischthys,* and even fire-colored megalodon emerged. The few great beasts that were left to hold the line for King Blu's army of the ocean turned and saw the monsters emerging from the sea portal. Megalodon led the attacks. The results were swift, peppering the sea with still more blood. Mechanical whales, whose whole bodies were littered with scales and teeth, launched at the other sea beasts. The larger animals of King Blu's army retreated further into the deeper recesses of the ocean. The dragons let up a fiery cry.

Steel Wings looked as the dragons danced across the sky. But even the falcon knew: Feng was right. A momentary victory was only delaying the inevitable. The Army of The Black Ocean was quite simply the greatest, largest animal army to ever exist. Their numbers were the stuff of fables. And if those armies failed, there was always their master. The last time King Blu breached, the entire ocean changed course, the animal empress went mad, and every animal enemy within two suns' swim had died.

Yet, the animal lords had won the day. Even if it was only one brief flicker in the fires of Time, that standing flame had to count for something.

CHAPTER 5

Animus Nor
Nunavut, Canada

The statue stared back at Moon Herald, half-formed, with only one complete paw and one fully chiseled eye. With the news of war, Thunder Killer had sent eagles to each of the animal kingdoms of *Animus Nor*. The eagle king declared from his mountain perch that all able animals must fortify the kingdom against the rising tides. And so, Cave Sun and the attending animals left the sculpture to attend to a much larger undertaking. Still, Moon Herald felt haunted by the spirit of his forebear, unable to show the cunning or experience of the great white wolf. The surviving wolf factions barely listened. They squabbled among themselves—the gray wolves against the Timberwolves and white wolves—over which faction should lead. Moon Herald managed to tackle, bite, and subdue each head wolf. But fangs alone did not make a wolf a leader.

Up in the sky, circling the clouds, was the omen that brought the nascent leader of the wolf pack out of The Great Mother Den. The vast, arched wings, tipped with the colors of night, were unmistakable. These were the wings of the blindingly white snowy owl. It was as if the spirit of the sky took the form of a bird, with eyes as yellow-black and ancient as Time itself. The young wolf leader arched his gray-white head to see the prophet of the heavens. Catching the eyes of the tundra wolves keeping guard was another figure, a giant pinkish shell with tree trunks for legs, slowly marching forward.

"Moon Herald," Sky Prophet said upon descending beneath the great granite statue. "Have you eaten well in the last moon cycle? The night of our departure is at hand."

"Master owl," Moon Herald said, in a way that made Snow Prophet feel even more ancient than he was. "I have come to greet you and to tell you that I cannot leave. The wolves I command are restless. One wolf house pounces upon another. At least two other wolf rivals clamor to be called the king. When you lose a great mother," Moon Herald said, looking up at the shadow of the statue overhead, "the younger pups come out to test themselves. If I leave now, I will be seen as abdicating my throne."

Snow Prophet shook the cold from his wings. His yellow-black eyes settled on the young wolf in front of him, so full of insecurities. "Physical power may get a wolf to the throne," he said, "but only the bludgeoning of Time makes a true king. Moon Shadow knew this when she hunted down the great serpent empress. Your wolves will know this too, in time."

"But why must I come personally?" Moon Herald asked. "There are many Alaskan tundra wolves and Eastern wolves just waiting for the chance to prove themselves."

"But there is only one wolf the goddess will speak to," Snow Prophet said. "The wolf of her choosing, the one who is appointed to succeed her."

"Enough!" the lumbering tortoise called from the background. "I've swam in the same tides as the whale god himself. You expect me to stop walking because of a little yelping on the part of some dogs? Out of my way. I march forward."

"Please forgive the forwardness of my friend," Snow Prophet said. "In a thousand years, the great tortoise has learned many things. Unfortunately, good manners are not among the number."

Moon Herald howled. The howl had the ferocity, if not the fullness, of that of his predecessor. Still, it was enough to quiet the tundra wolves on guard.

"That's better," Criddock said, lumbering along. "Make some room for the old boy, young pups."

Moon Herald watched as Criddock the Cudgel approached Snow Prophet and the old friends greeted one another.

"Every time I think you can go no slower, you still find a way to astonish me," Snow Prophet said.

"Which of us has to contend with the forces of a mad whale bent on destroying everything that crawls?" Criddock asked. "Not all animals can simply fly away from the fight, Oracle of the North. Some of us live in it."

Snow Prophet shook his plumed head at the rebuff and turned to face the uncertain wolf.

"Criddock's words," Snow Prophet said, "while they may seem like the complaints of an old fossil of an animal, are why he is here. The ancient tortoise has the power to blind the powers of the ocean, ever so slightly, to the doings of the land. If our mission is to succeed, it is imperative that King Blu cannot see what we are doing."

"For once, Snow Prophet is right," Criddock said. "I was among the first animals to receive the *rulku* magic in the ocean. It operated differently in me before the nanobots evolved. Some of those early powers are with me still. So long as I am near you, if not exactly caught up with you, you are safe. So why the sad eyes, Master Wolf?"

Moon Herald shook his mane.

"The young wolf king does not wish to go," Snow Prophet said. "He fears losing his throne to rivals."

"There is much work to be done among the wolf kingdoms," Moon Herald said.

"There will be no work if King Blu has his way," Criddock replied. The old tortoise turned his green-scaled head and beady black-purple eyes upon his friend. "Perhaps Snow Prophet and I can show you what the world of *Animus Nor* will soon face, if you still need convincing, young king. The lands of *Yv-ot-Sing* are already besieged and may soon fall. After that, we will all face the same fate."

Snow Prophet nodded. The two mages came together. Criddock used his nanobots to create a holographic ocean, with a predator of pure black and large, fiery eyes. Wherever the creature swam, death followed. Sharks and seals and even great octopi knelt before the passing of the whale god. Snow Prophet gave the holographic image an aerial view. Above the waters where King Blu domi-nated sat *Animus Nor.* Quarreling wolves shook the fur from their legs in fear of the mounting ocean tide. Gigantic quakes and tsunamis assailed the land. Soon, wolf pups yelped as shark lords devoured them. Animal after animal drowned until the water was the color of wolf blood. Nothing in the den of the great mother, Moon Shadow, survived. Even the mighty statue washed away.

Moon Herald looked on, shaking. "How long do we have?" the wolf king asked.

"As soon as Feng falls, the tides rise," Snow Prophet said.

"King Blu is a great but ruthless monarch," Criddock said. "He meant to humble the dragon emperor for delaying his plans of conquest in a show of might to any animal lords who would oppose his will. That act of vengeance is the only reason we are alive now. So I suggest we get moving. Are we agreed, young lord?"

Moon Herald took in a deep breath of tundra air. The wolf king nodded.

"There is only one tiny matter," Snow Prophet said. "We don't know exactly where we're going."

"What?!" Criddock asked. "You old fool! You invite a tortoise to crawl on land, for many a moon cycle, mind you, and you don't have the intellect to figure out where we're going first? I thought you were a prophet. Isn't the title in your very name?"

"Not even King Dryga knows for sure," Snow Prophet said. "Thunder Killer's eagles last saw Freyda The Fatal heading north. Ice Giant searched and found nothing. King Dryga called his greatest general back. The search is left to us."

"Isn't there some portal that the mouse fellow could give us? The one that seems to live unusually long for such a tiny creature?" Criddock asked.

"Freyda has used her magic to stay hidden," Snow Prophet said. "Pale Ghost's great-grandchildren worked with him many nights, and unfortunately, no one could overcome the bear witch's magic. That's why we have a wolf."

"I can only track that which I sense," Moon Herald said.

"But the one who guides you can track more," Snow Prophet said, looking the wolf king in his uncertain eyes. "I sense Moon Shadow is with you, seeking to communicate. She will show us the way. She may even show us The Firebird."

"You pinned all our hopes on a wolf's dreams?" Criddock asked. "Maybe King Blu is right about a lack of intelligence on the land."

"I feel her presence," Snow Prophet said. "Soon, you will too."

Criddock shook his massive, oblong head. "Let's get going, then. Time is scarce," he said. "Lead us, owl prophet. Try not to call too much attention to yourself, and maybe we will follow."

<hr />

Rul-Seerus

Mount Asgard
Nunavut, Canada

Thunder Killer sat on his perch among the king of mountains. All around, the great eagle clans circled, stirring up fresh clouds. The wise old king of *Animus Nor* eyed a golden storm on the horizon, one that felt like a great feathered sun.

"What is it—a living beast or a *rulku* monstrosity?" Thunder Killer asked Pale Thunder.

"It is a judgment from the whale god," Pale Thunder answered. "It is fire from the belly of the sea, all wrapped up in a living sun."

"The *rulku* files once spoke of this," Thunder Killer said. "They said it was a fire of the heavens that took out the terror lizards that ruled before the *rulku* overlords ascended. I think they might have called it a fire rock."

Thunder Killer's eyes saw the dancing fire almost immediately extending from a great sulfur ball like a misshapen tongue. "Flee," he cried to Pale Thunder, Sunfire and Death Talon, his commanders. "Order the eagles and hawks to defend themselves. This sun moves to strike down the perch of *Rul-Seerus* itself."

"But why?" Pale Thunder asked.

"To melt the ice. To make more sea," Thunder Killer said. "Fly—now, my son!"

Great waves of birds of all colors, from the majestic sodden brown of the hawk to the bright white crests of the noble eagles, filled the skies. All around them, able birds, from the snowy owls to the puffins, auks, and terns, made the white sky canvas yellow, red, and black. It was as if the sky were pulling off its own skin to release blood from a wound—so quickly did the birds flee the scorching second sun.

"Gather the thunderbirds," Thunder Killer said. "We must divert the fire rock!"

As the eagle soldiers gathered around their general and king, fear feasted upon their eyes. A few openly shrieked in terror at whatever the plague winds held. Every eagle knew: They were there only to buy time for the other sky and land animals to flee.

Thunder Killer flapped his wings and spoke. "It has been said by our ancestors that not even the greatest wind can kill an eagle," the noble king said. "Today, we shall see. I fly before you now as the lord of *Animus Nor,* but I am not as I once was. My wings are tinged with the scars of battle. The fire of previous conquests has burned the feathers of my wings. My bones bristle with age and beg for rest. Even my cry rivals the thunder less and less each day. Yet, I carry the heart of all eagles who flew before me, and what a mighty heart that is! The eagle ancestors are in my blood, stirring that heart as I speak. And they cry out in righteous fury for the glory of deeds undone! Their spirits remind me now that the skies have known no majesty greater than an eagle in flight. The winds have known no mightier wing. That is why the whale god targets us: to lord over the eagles, the hawks, the owls, and the terns is to lord over the skies. But I say, today this old eagle king shows a god a thing or two about who truly rules the skies! I say that today this old general becomes the strike of lightning and the crash of thunder! Fight with me now, eagles! Bleed with me, hawks, owls, and terns! If this sun is the last I shall ever see, let my cry shatter the heavens and let my spirit set fire to the sea! And when animals look back, ages hence, let them say, in fiery wonder: There was a flight of eagles once that made the sky shake and the sun cower!"

The eagles rallied, flapping their wings and shrieking in valor.

The birds flew at full might at the rock that would decimate *Animus Nor.* Thunder Killer led a battalion of eagles, flanked by Death Talon, Pale Thunder, and the hawks on one side and Sunfire and the thunderbirds on the other. The owls and the terns approached from above. The hurtling rock spat fire as it descended in its golden aureole. Yet, Thunder Killer showed no fear. The cries of the eagles, hawks, and owls shook the nanobots until they shattered. The crashing talons of eagles, thunderbirds and owls pushed the fire rock, steering it to the waters below. Eagles, hawks, owls, terns, thunderbirds, and half of the birds in Creation flew at the fire rock with their very lives. The collisions and cries took their toll on the rock until it broke off over the sea. Small bits of the rock crashed everywhere, some over the open ocean, some over *Animus Nor.* The birds immediately ripped at any plague nanobots that jumped from the fiery wreck or rock. A frenzy of birds destroyed as many nanobots as an eagle's eye could see.

And yet, in the frenzy, Pale Thunder circled the waters, searching. His eagle eye spotted a feather in flames. Pale Thunder raced to the sea. His beak lifted the fiery feather–for no more of its mighty king's body was left. Pale Thunder flew around in great, cascading circles for all the eagles to see: even the fire paid testimony to their fallen eagle king.

CHAPTER 6

Yvot-Sing
Beijing, China

At first, the victory was too sweet to the eyes of the war-worn dragon emperor to see the truth of the waters. Yet, after seeing the greatest of the *leedischthys* cease in its movements, its silvery green fins detaching and falling to the ocean floor, the truth was undeniable. There was something else stirring in the waters, something mightier than a megalodon, more massive than even the largest of the mechanical, toothed whales. It was the ocean itself, creeping up in tidal waves tall enough to knock against the wings of dragons. Feng had heard tell of such a moveable ocean once before. It could be none other than the whale god itself.

Sure enough, whirling clouds of miscreation stirred overhead, reaching down to the tidal waves, creating a smothering storm of lightning-laced fury. The sky and sea grew inseparable, all pummeling at the dragon-fired wall that held the line between Thraxis' ancient army and this Armada of the Black Ocean.

"Steady your wings," Feng ordered. "Whatever you do, don't look the whale god in the eyes."

"The whale god—here?" Alazar the Red asked. The tone of the ferocious dragon was like that of a scurrying gecko seeing its tiny life flashing in the flames before its eyes.

"Hold firm," Feng said in a fiery growl. "Fly high. Fight the wind and sea currents. Once they pass, we have our chance to end this war. The whale god only strikes once. If we don't kill King Blu, the animal world may never have another chance."

Thrysta and Fyvol saw the dimming fire in each other's eyes, but the noble dragons held firm.

The winds sparked, speaking in strange tongues at once ancient and divine. The skies became swirling black waves, and the swirling black waves of the sea became a naked canvas of lightning. No bird or dragon could tell which was which: sky, sea, or land. It was as if the world returned to an age of primordial thunder. So the sea of preternatural life stirred, as if at first creation, from the black womb of a motherless universe.

"I am death and life," the thunder said. "None come to this world but through me."

The dragons looked at each other. Feng heard that voice, at once crackling with age and newborn with fire, once before. Soon enough, from the lightning-laced clouds, he saw the skeleton form of Yu The Golden Nightmare carved out in furious light. The lightning changed form again, like a dancing beast pivoting upon an uneven dance floor. Yu The Golden Nightmare became the face of thousands of creatures, from ravenous vultures to Moon Shadow, cast in fire, to Azaz, a massive bear's skull made of cloud and thunder.

"You are not my children," the thunder said, striking a still deeper chord. "You are Abomination. All abominations must be destroyed."

Flying out from the clouds were Mother Raven and the other Night Eye crows, fire lacing their wings. Somehow, the raven lords were at once dead and alive, fleshly but reborn with soulless white eyes.

"Fly, fatherless dragons," The Night Eye advised. "Time is not your ally. Only Death calls from these winds. And on its tongue is a single command: the great Leviathan, the whale god of this and all ages, allows you the privilege of choosing your own death."

"We choose to die with the flesh of the whale god in our talons, with the fire of the dragon scorching King Blu's very eyes," Feng said. "*Yvot-Sing* belongs to me. It is my treasure to hoard and no other's. Its animals are sacred to me. Enough wasting of words with traitors and underlings. Let the whale god reveal himself, and we shall show him the true meaning of death."

Feng took a deep, rumbling breath, as did the rest of The Dragon Guard. Seconds later, a new lightning took to the sky, dragon fire striking down upon The Night Eye. The bird prophets burned, only to disappear into the clouds, and reappear, otherworldly and unharmed.

At the gong of fresh thunder, cyclones formed. The dragons fought off the fierce winds, only to gaze ever so briefly upon King Blu himself. The godly Leviathan, easily the size of two blue whales put together, breached the fires. The sight was like no other: teeth of a *basilosaurus*, the mass of a great blue whale, the cranium dwarfing that of pod upon pod of sperm whales, and the black and white stripes of an orca against a massive blue body made almost entirely of deathly light. In the pupil of the eyes sat the entire globe, all of Creation, in miniature, circling in pale fire.

"I created *Yvot-Sing*," King Blu said, in a whale song so mighty it shook the skies until every spark of light shattered. "The animal dead belong to me."

Feng set his dancing red eyes firmly upon the exposed back of the great whale god. "Now," he ordered The Dragon Guard. "Attack! Wreak havoc until the flesh of the whale god bloodies your talons and feeds your fangs!"

The dragon emperor, flanked by Fyvol, Alazar, and Thrysta, flew straight into the cyclone, right for the whale god.

Up King Blu came from the heart of the ocean, releasing the song that first brought death to the world. Its notes were clangs of godly thunder, punctuated by crackles of ancient ashen fire. The very vibration of the cry rattled the stars and punctured the clouds until every animal within one thousand leagues fell through the eye of the cyclone to the savage sea. Even the mighty Dragon Guard was not immune. Feng, Fyvol, Alazar, and Thrysta fell through their own wall of dragon fire, crashing to the foundations of the world.

King Blu breached again. Just like that, *Yvot-Sing* was no more.

Vol Tylon

The Great Lakes, USA

The rising of the ocean, crushing the land of *Yvot-Sing* beneath it, was a tale only the birds could tell. And tell it they did. There was a mass migration of falcons, eagles, hawks, owls, geese, grebes, flamingos, and waterfowl, so much so that a rainbow-hued cloud blocked out any last vestiges of sun. Among the number was Steel Wings, who flew ahead—days, nights, or whatever blackness they blurred into. Steel Wings made it to the kingdom of Seerus-*Ungalore,* where the sparrows, nighthawks, snow geese, and sandpipers all heard the tale. The seabirds took the news with their flight, and before Snow Prophet knew it, Orij was again on his trail. The higher the great snowy owl flew, the more the black hawk set its eyes upon his. Snow Prophet perched atop an ancient peak of *Sygrie,* once called the Huron Mountains in the forbidden *rulku* tongue.

"Oracle," Orij said. "This time I have news for you."

The strained notes in the hawk's shrill cry did not bode well. Snow Prophet shook the iciness from his wings and settled in to hear. "So, it's begun," Snow Prophet said.

"What, master owl?" Orij asked.

"The Great Flood," Snow Prophet said. "Since our ancestors first flew from the sea, the oracles have feared such a day. I feared the *rulku* more."

"Fear the whale god," Orij said. "King Blu attacked Feng directly. The entire Dragon Guard, holding up against the assault of Admiral Xrata, fell through their wall of fire. The whale god breached once and sucked them into the sea. King Blu breached twice, and the ocean consumed the land. We have no idea how many animals are still living. The birds did not stay for long. We flew through the death cloud for *Seerus-Ungalore*. Only The Night Eye remained to reign in the stead of the whale god."

"Then our time is short," Snow Prophet said. The great owl closed its eyes, concentrating on the energy flowing through the sky. Through the fear, rage, and death, there was a deafening silence, a great emptiness where before there had been life.

"I sense very few survivors," Snow Prophet said. "And *Seerus-Ungalore* may be next. Join us, Orij. We quest for the only witch who still holds enough magic to help us face the whale god."

"Who is this we?" Orij asked.

"A wolf one sun behind me, and a giant tortoise over five suns away," Snow Prophet said. "The wolf will slumber soon. I can sense the spirit of Moon Shadow running with him. Tonight, the wolf goddess will speak."

Orij nodded. "I have nowhere else to fly," he said. "I come only in warning: Protect your lands if you can."

"Rest on this peak, Orij," Snow Prophet said. "We must awaken the wolf spirit. Let us pray and hunt and feast tonight. Tomorrow, the world may be a different place."

In the snowy patches behind the sunlit peaks, Moon Herald found a makeshift den of branches and rock that must have dated back to The Serpent War. Some animal scout, its blood still upon the rocks, facing rattlers, anacondas, and terror lizards, made one last sanctuary before the hopeless battle. Moon Herald felt the same fear tonight. While the *Osine* was broken, with spots of dialect from local birds across the mountains, the message was clear. A bird had appeared before Snow Prophet and announced: A chunk of the world was no more. How long might it be before King Blu crested the waves of nearer oceans? Moon Herald circled, clearing the snow drifts. He rested his gray-white head. Within moments, the exhausted wolf felt himself drifting into an uneasy sleep.

At first, there were no such things as visions: just fragmented dreams, shadowy glimpses of sharks, the rows of serrated teeth on their extended jaws at the ready. There was the specter of a great black whale, almost like a whirlpool of darkness swallowing all the surrounding life in an unending ocean. And then there was a fire in mid-crackle. In the tongues of flame, Moon Herald saw an ancestral land of wolves. There was The Fire Wolf, the father of all wolves, and River Wolf, the mother of the Timberwolves of the North. They stood on either side of The Great Mother of all wolves, Moon Shadow, who walked with Sun Shadow and two fire pups, taking shape among shadow and flame.

"Mother wolf," Moon Herald said in his sleep. "Are you really here? How I wish you were still alive! How I wish you were still our mother!"

Moon Shadow stood, a wolf of white fire now, the one wolf who outran The Fire Wolf.

"I am always your mother," Moon Shadow said, "and the mother to all wolves. That is why I appear to you now. Treacherous birds spy on you," the spirit wolf said. "Even now, some show loyalty to The Night Eye, whose witchery joins them to the god of death."

"*Yvot-Sing* is no more. I fear we are next," Moon Herald said. "We must find this Freyda The Fatal to find The Firebird. We must trust one witch to overcome another."

"Oceans rise, and oceans fall, but the spirit of life is a thing that goes on forever," Moon Shadow said. "King Blu cannot extinguish it fully. His twin, *Avrah*, guides and protects you. Against the whale god, there is no victory. You cannot stand against him, not even with Freyda, not even with The Firebird. Snow Prophet and Sky Death cannot advise a winning strategy to stand against death. Only *Avrah* can stop him."

"Then what must we do?" Moon Herald asked. "Where must we go?"

"Before the second moon," Moon Shadow said, from the blinding fire, "King Blu will strike again. He shall strike the remaining lands at once, but there are some animal lords he seeks more than others. King Dryga and Klang Krugal shall be first. Any original animal lords and oracles, like Snow Prophet, Sky Death, and Zulta, will follow. Even Methuselah and The Firebird shall be hunted. Each animal lord was not born solely of *rulku* magic but of the will of *Avrah*. *Avrah* separated her great mothering spirit into each of the animal lords. Only if the spirits of the animal lords stand together with Methuselah will Avrah regain her full form and be able to vanquish King Blu. King Blu will go to any lengths to stop this until he recreates the world in his image."

"But how can we accomplish this?" Moon Herald asked.

"After the great deluge, when King Blu proclaims victory, the time will be short," Moon Shadow said. "That is when you must face King Blu in the land most difficult for him to claim, the land of *Gola Dwyn*. Only when the whale god is fully ready will he assault the land whose magic nearly rivals his own.

To face him, you will need all the animal lords, even those like Feng, who have been made into servants of the whale god."

The fire spun in tiny flames, melting into the sky.

"My time is short," Moon Shadow said. "Until the time is at hand, the gods may not interfere with the living. Animals must prove themselves worthy. Find Freyda. Ask her to announce what I have said to all animals, through what magic she has left. Have her bring you to King Dryga. He shall protect you in the battle ahead. Freyda must join with Snow Prophet and Methuselah. Only with the magic of all animal lords can Avrah rise."

"But Mother Wolf, I am so weak," Moon Herald said. "I am not you. Who will believe me?"

"You are the wolf I have appointed for this task," Moon Shadow said. "I run with you. Now go. Get up and run. There is no time to rest. Gather your friends and head to *Fyng-Thilkore*, Mount Silverthrone. Freyda practices healing herself and her magic there. But be quick. The Night Eye sees far, and King Blu's threat extends still farther."

With that, the white fire raged, consuming all the animals of the ancestral lands until there was nothing but moonlight. Moon Herald got up to run, only to find that Snow Prophet and another bird were circling the skies less than a half sun ahead. Spotting the wolf, they flew closer until they could make out the Timberwolf's stampeding paws.

"*Fyng-Thilkore,*" Moon Herald said. "We must hurry!"

"Run, then, wolf king," Snow Prophet said. "I shall fly and tell Criddock. Orij shall round up some eagles and hawks. Perhaps they can help us carry the oracle with us, for protection."

Up ahead, Moon Herald saw a pack of fiery wolves of white, red, gold, and gray. He knew: His ancestors led the way. And so, Moon Herald ran as never before, like a wolf carrying fire on his back.

CHAPTER 7

Unslyg, Gola-Dwyn
The Amazon Rainforest

Aeyra smelt the fragrance of his mother in the leaves of the dense jungles. That smell was a potent potpourri of fear and power. The boy turned half-man, half-beast marveled that the most beautiful places on Earth were also the most deadly. At any turn, a snake lord or poison dart frog might take his life. Yet, there was something stirring the young mage warrior, a calling that he could not articulate. It was as if, the moment he saw even a reflection of the eyes of the whale god on the open sea, Death had seeped through his pores and mingled with his blood. And now, it was as if Death were ripping at his veins, seeking to get out. Long had Aeyra meditated in the mountains upon his purpose. Now, Aeyra knew how ungodly his purpose was and how forlorn. Yet, he walked through the dense jungle anyway, seeking the darkest prison cell of all.

"Turn away now," Bryne, the boa guard, ordered, "or I will crush the life out of you."

Aeyra stood for a moment, removing the hood of dead animal skins that had protected him in the harsh jungle. Bryne looked upon the young man beast, recognizing the one so favored by his fallen empress.

"You," Bryne said. "The cursed child, now grown. Go. The crazy witch queen cannot save you now."

"Groth the Impaler," Aeyra said. "He's in the cell you hide, is he not—in a winding snake path, deep underground?"

The boa guard hissed. In that hiss was a hint of laughter. "What could you possibly want with a wolverine lord, boy?"

Bryne slithered closer, right where he could drop and wrap himself around Aeyra's neck: an easy kill. Aeyra watched the boa coil, standing his ground.

"Groth The Impaler was a faithful servant of The Night Eye, the ones who opposed your mother's rule. You seek his death, don't you?" Bryne asked.

"I am a man of horrible destiny," Aeyra said, taking out a metallic laser gun from the age of the *rulku*. "I seek many things. Slither aside or see my destiny with your own eyes."

Bryne dropped from the dense branches of the Kapok tree, ready to strike. Aeyra caught the massive boa in one extended arm. The two creatures fought, the boa coiling with all its might, forcing Aeyra's gun to the ground. Aeyra fought to dispel the predator with a gentle prick of his finger. Bryne looked into the eyes of the mad *rulku* abomination and crashed through the earth, into an underground chamber. There, several pit vipers and Amazon coral snakes slithered up towards the interloper. Aeyra simply watched.

"These eyes have seen the whale god and lived," Aeyra announced as the snakes grew unbearably close. "Slither away or see what I saw."

The pit vipers, yellow-green and deadly, struck at the *rulku* that was *rulku* and not *rulku* at one and the same time. Their fangs bared, showing, in languid green drips, strange, pointed tips that Thraxis gave to her troops in The Serpent War. Aeyra's eyes grew white as the skies before a storm. The vipers lunged. Aeyra picked up and aimed his laser gun. In sundry rapid shots, he laid waste to the attacking vipers. Their bodies fell. In their dying moments, the vipers blocked the way to the snake pit below. Aeyra walked over their fallen bodies as Bryne regained the last of his strength. Bryne slithered with all his might to wrap his gargantuan green body around the neck of the man-beast warrior. Aeyra grabbed the snake's head, pulling Bryne's eyes to his. In his eyes, he saw the fiery, globe-like pupils of the whale god emerge.

"You're a prophet of King Blu," Bryne said, in his last breaths. "You betray your own people, faithless *rulku* beast."

"I have been given a terrible gift," Aeyra said, bending down to speak to the dying snake guard in the tongue of the snakes. "It is a gift I must share with the world."

Aeyra ascended, only to see the pit vipers guarding the way to Groth down beneath the roots of even the tallest trees of the Amazon. Aeyra pulled up the prickly vines sealing off the entrance. All as one, the snakes, hydralike, attacked. Aeyra fired enough shots to drop the flying body of wriggling serpents to the soil. They slithered to attack again, but Aeyra only turned his gaze on them and meditated in his stare. The serpents hissed their last breaths as Aeyra looked upon their bodies. The sacredness of death was not lost upon him.

Aeyra descended into the pit, right up to the door of stone that held the wolverine inside. The man beast pried at the stone fruitlessly until he saw a simple lever on the ground designed to be opened by the weight of a snake. Aeyra dragged Bryne's body towards the lever. Recognizing the weight of its master, the lever gave. The stone rolled aside. Inside, an emaciated old wolverine made momentary eye contact. The wolverine lunged at Aeyra. Aeyra grabbed hold of the wolverine and looked him in the eyes.

"Thraxis' son," Groth said.

"Wolverine god," Aeyra said.

"Let me live," Groth said, "and I shall help you in your quest."

"The only way for you to live is for you to die," Aeyra said. "Look in my eyes, wolverine lord, and see the truth."

Groth let out a fierce growl at whatever picture the burning eyes revealed. The wolverine lord let out his last breath. Aeyra bent down and stroked Groth's fur, comforting the dying lord.

"You were the heart of the gods," Aeyra said, "beating in one small, fierce body. Rest now, wolverine lord. Glory in your death. The time for you to rise will come soon enough."

Aeyra stepped back, only to see the fire spirit emerge from the wolverine. The fire wolverine, dripping in white, red, and gold flames, looked at the man beast for a moment. In a whirlwind of flame, the fire wolverine ran off. Aeyra knew where he ran but did not run after the wolverine spirit. Instead, he took out a long, serrated knife. Aeyra skinned the fallen wolverine. He cleaned the fur in a nearby river and put it upon his shoulders. He then buried the body, knelt, and said a prayer to the *rulku* gods. With that, Aeyra rose, following his destiny as he might a river snake.

Animus Nor

Nunavut, Canada

A third plague took to the trees of *Animus Nor* the way The Second Plague Monster reduced the population. This plague was minute, unseen and unfelt. Only when the crops the animal kingdoms depended on faltered did the turkeys cry out. Even the very best crops the nanobots harvested grew brown and crackling. The poisoned foliage upset the intricate communication of the plant world but also killed entire populations of caribou, gray squirrels, and American beavers. Even the bluebirds, thrushes and yellow-rumped warblers fell from the sky. To kill an animal is to kill the foundation of the ecological world; to kill a plant is to kill the world itself. Entire ecosystems of freshly awakened and unawakened animals fell, polluting rivers and forests, keeping King Dryga, the new regent of Animus Nor after Thunder Killer's fall, busy day and night. The eagles mapped out the spread of the contagion while Pale Ghost and his great-grandchildren fought valiantly to undo the evil magic of the whale god, magic worthy only of the *rulku*.

Meanwhile, the waters rose to unnatural heights. Always, the eyes of the sharks were upon the animals of the land, circling in a sea of mist and blood. The hammerheads and great white sharks, under the cruel Admiral Xrata, swam in mystical waves, preparing to mount their offenses. The orcas, under the fearsome Wylaka, who had seen more kills than any living whale except for King Blu himself, held the perimeter. Ice Giant, servant of the high bear king, and his fellow polar bears, used the magic of fire to keep the orcas from encroaching further. Yet, the sea was nothing if not persistent. At any moment, the mere presence of the whale god might signal the same wave of doom for *Animus Nor* as for *Yvot-Sing*.

Death Talon, chief of the hawks, circled King Dryga, seeking answers. "The seabirds speak of the sunken kingdom of the dragon lords."

"And of Thunder Killer?" King Dryga asked.

"Not a single bird has a report," Death Talon said. "Too much fear penetrates even the hearts of the eagles. The plants die. Animals die with them. Birds say that our time of death is at hand."

King Dryga, his few white hairs speckling his magnificent grizzly coat of earth-red and forest-brown, stood surveying the danger with the most elite of his Blood Paw.

"Legend has it the great eagle king of the North once spoke of how to beat a serpent," King Dryga said. "You lift the creature up by its writhing body, tear it, and then drop its remains to the hard rock below."

"But a whale is not a serpent, my lord," Death Talon said. "Especially a cunning whale, who seizes the food from our very mouths."

"True, but a whale is also not a land dweller," King Dryga said. "With The Night Eye, the whale god gains power over the skies. His legions control the outermost lands. My father's blood burns in me, and it would fight. Yet, my colder king's blood tells me that a fight against an insuperable foe is no fight at all. Start evacuations of the land. Move all creatures that crawl, run, or fly to the heart of *Gol-Kilpyne*. Even the power of the whale god pales there. Not a single portal stands. No plague seizes the upper plants. *Gol-Kilpyne* is where we will make our fortress until the march to the final battle."

"How can you be so sure, my lord?" Death Talon asked. "Might this not be King Blu's plan—to unite us and then destroy us with one giant wave?"

King Dryga stood looking at his lost kingdom, out to the cold eyes of the sea, into the eyes of Admiral Xrata himself.

"It is his plan," King Dryga said. "The blood of the sea speaks his plan plainly to us. But the mountains will protect us. I feel an old magic calling me back there, the magic of the banished Mother Bear. In the whispers of whipping winds, her words lacerate my ears. The whale god has a blind spot, and we must exploit it. Now, hurry. Tell as many creatures of The Great Migration as birds can before the throat of the smallest warbler is hoarse. We meet our common fate together."

Death Talon flew off, shrieking out orders in the sky. King Dryga turned away from Admiral Xrata.

"One day," the voice of Azaz whispered, "I will pluck you from the waters and feed on your liver as you writhe, begging to die."

Yet, King Dryga leashed the fire within. The great bear king turned back, leading the migration westward, before the killing waters came.

CHAPTER 8

Fyng-Thilkore
Mount Silverthrone

In the sliver of sky not yet eaten by the thunderclouds, Snow Prophet saw a speck below him. Snows yet clung to the rocky cliffs; mighty sequoia treetops still swung in ice and breeze, yet from his elevation just below the clouds, Snow Prophet saw Moon Herald running. The stolid Timberwolf's body cascaded up and down in the drifts, fighting to keep above the unmelted snow. Yet, just ahead, after many bright suns of trekking, was the icy monolith that stood like a lost god just below the stars: *Fyng-Thilkore*. Snow Prophet saw another speck, larger than the first, surrounded by smoke and flame, charging towards them. He swooped down between the two. The massive bear mother stood fully upright on her hind legs, staring.

"Great Mother Bear," Snow Prophet said. "We have searched these many moons to find you. The earth is hard, and the sky is cold, but the sea is harder and colder still. Your son, King Dryga, faces an impossible battle against the whale god. We have come for your help."

"My help," Freyda the Fatal, white with snow, said. "My son is his own king. He does not welcome the priestess of Azaz. He exiled his own mother," the bear witch added, with something of a smile. "A mighty king he has become."

"You yet have a role to play," Snow Prophet said. "Methuselah the Witch Tree heals. She cannot conjure as she once did, saving her power for the final hour. You are the most powerful witch yet alive. Only you can bring together those that war and strife cast apart."

"So your friend tells me," Freyda said, continuing in her hunt.

"Moon Herald, king of the wolves, comes to beg you," Snow Prophet said. "Famine grips the land."

"Not the wolf. Your other friend," Freyda said, turning around.

There, beyond all possibility, stood the great green and pink shell that Snow Prophet knew so well. He had missed the sight, so focused was he on the fire and smoke that signaled the bear queen. Yet, there the tortoise was, looking strangely comfortable in the northern snows.

"How did you get here so suddenly, old friend?" Snow Prophet asked. "What bird could lift such a rock and fly so fast?"

"One of us had to use his mind," Criddock the Cudgel said. "It figures that it would have to be me."

Looking closer, Snow Prophet saw the truth. The ancient tortoise had not traveled at all to the forbidding ice of *Fyng-Thilkore*. He had simply meditated, using his power to reach out to the soul of the mother bear.

"The tortoise prophet has explained the matter well," Freyda said. "What you seek has never been done. Yet, with all of our magic combined, it may be possible."

Snow Prophet arched his head, studying his friend for answers.

"In the song of the whales," Criddock said, "which stretches the length of the great sea, the legend of King Blu is well-known. So, too, is the song of *Avrah*, his fellow goddess. In the whale song, only King Blu came in the flesh to live among his creatures. *Avrah* took the form of the sun and the sky, or the *eeee-raaa*, as the whales call that which is beyond the sea. Yet, my meditations told me differently. King Blu took but one mighty body, one so powerful no animal lord could stand against him. *Avrah*, however, split herself between all of her creations."

"The animal lords," Snow Prophet said.

Criddock nodded. "The voice of *Avrah*, the only song powerful enough to counter the death song of King Blu," he added, "can only be sung if the souls of *Avrah* join together again behind a manifestation of the goddess. The magic of Freyda can bring the animal lords into unison, as she once did with Dryga and Azaz. Then, *Avrah*, who is already among us, will remember her true form and rise."

"That makes perfect sense," Snow Prophet said. "The only answer to a whale song of ungodly destruction can be another song, that of creation. So you'll help us?" Snow Prophet asked.

"I will help you to help my son," Freyda said. "Even in exile, I am his mother."

At that moment, the Timberwolf arrived, greeting the great bear with a lyrical howl of his own.

"You needn't bother," Snow Prophet told him. "Criddock beat us here."

"The strange tortoise?" Moon Herald asked.

"None other," Snow Prophet answered.

"But how?" Moon Herald asked.

"Magic." Snow Prophet shook the weariness from his wings. "Of course, the mercurial tortoise could have told us this and saved us an unnecessary journey."

"Every journey is necessary," Criddock said. "From each step, the soul grows."

"Grows tired, hungry, and near-dead, you mean," Snow Prophet said.

"Faithless oracle," Criddock said. "Do you really believe I would hurt my friends? My magic is only so strong. Soon, my visage will fade. That is why you must lead Freyda back to *Animus Nor,* back to the throne of King Dryga. There, in the heart of the rocky earth, the animal lords will prepare for the inevitable. Can you do that much correctly?"

"There my vision fails me," Snow Prophet said.

"But not mine," Moon Herald said. "I could do so one-hundred more times, if it would save my wolves."

"Spoken like a true king," Criddock said.

"Let us get fire and warmth then–for tomorrow, we fly," Snow Prophet said.

Freyda led the ice-beleaguered owl and wolf to the warmth of her magical fire. Never had a witch's hearth looked so comforting.

Animus Nor

Nunavut, Canada

Over the craggy white peaks of ice, just near the waters, the eagles flew one last rotation in the skies. They were not commanders or lords, like Death Talon, lord of the hawks, or Pale Thunder, son of the lost high king of *Animus Nor.* They were not nobility, like Sky Death, the mightiest of vultures' clans. No, they were the elderly eagles, soldiers of The Serpent War. They were not strong enough, even after The Great Awakening, to fly in The Great Migration ordered by King Dryga, the new high king of *Animus Nor.* And so, they flew and circled, gathering the last of the sun in the storms that assailed them, as Sky Death and Thunder Killer had a generation ago, upon the passing of the great wolf queen.

"You are our brother and our king," the head eagle chorister cried.

"You once said the heart of all eagles beats in you," the eagles replied. "And what a mighty heart it is! So do our hearts beat in you, Thunder Killer, in this, our final hour. Let us be your elegy, great eagle king, as you sing ours!"

"Today we gather the sun from the storm clouds," the head chorister said, "in honor of the noblest eagle of them all, in honor of all eagles that have ever flown the sky. We gather the light for all the eagles yet to be born–for all the eagles yet to fly the skies. For the eagle ancestors reborn in us shall live again in them. We shall shatter the sky with our death cry, and they shall be our birth cry."

"We have become the crash of lightning, the cry of thunder," the eagles replied, circling with the clouds. "Today, make way, great heavens! The spirits of thousands of eagles come to you, angel birds of the unending skies! Every day we greet the rising sun, gathering sunlight for the dark days ahead. Today, we call upon the gathered sun to light our way into the *Zolyta*, to ask the great wind to take us to the skies of the worlds beyond worlds. Today is a great time to live, but an even greater time to die," the eagles called out in incantation, staring at the advancing storms.

The winds, with all of King Blu's wrath, came at them–winding, twisty tornados of white ice, of clouds so black and so white they blinded all with their darkness and with their light. There was lightning snaking from the sky. Thunder shook the firmaments and the wings of every bird. Rains, tentacles of waters from the skies, punished the lands. And in it all, there were flights of eagles, determined to honor their fallen brother, adamant to sing the song of all eagles before they died.

"I am Clipped Wing, great sentry in The Serpent War," one eagle cried. "Brown Feather is my son, and Tree Weaver is my daughter! Know that we flew the sky–that we were a family bold, brilliant, and beautiful as the sun itself!"

"And I am Stone Beak, one of Thunder Killer's oldest captains," another eagle cried. "I fought many battles. I won some, lost more. But know, all that live, that my eagle nestlings, Mountain Snow and Flower Feather, were my true pride and joy! I am one lucky to have flown the sky of the great spirit eagles, fortunate enough to have been a father! I am one of many notes in the great, unending Song of Life!"

With that cry, the storm clouds came, swallowing the old eagles, along with thousands of other birds that circled, singing glorious notes of that same eternal song. Whether some lived or all died, what prophet can say? All that this prophet can write is that on that day, the eagles met their deaths with honor, with such a fierce cry that it made even the spirit of *Avrah* shudder and say, *That is what life should be. That is the reason I created the earth.*

CHAPTER 9

Gungsung Dor
Bear Mountain, Rockies, USA

The Great Migration, at last, was at an end. The muskoxen, elks, lynxes, and polar bears felt unfamiliar on the malleable soil of the Rocky highlands. Several animal tribes, like the Alaskan moose, sang songs of the ancient ice in the days before King Blu's mad assault. The Blood Paw, among the most formidable of foes in the past, welcomed visitors from the North and from the South. Special hawk emissaries, including the great Death Talon, lord of the hawks, and eagle lords, like Pale Thunder, son of the great Thunder Killer, took to the skies, surveying the remaining lands. The sea was in the sky, in whirling clouds leagues deep, threatening to overtake the native lands. The eagles and hawks searched frantically for any signs of portals the moose and bears might topple. All was eerily quiet, like death on a moonless night.

"My animals are in your debt, King Dryga," Igru, lord of the moose, said.

The giant moose had white fur hanging from his sturdy chin. Amazingly, time healed many scars from The Serpent War, but not those in the great moose's bones. Time had settled in, and Igru, while still fierce, was naturally slower than the young moose who outran the thunderbirds.

"Not even the *rulku* could take the fortress mountain of *Gungsung Dor*," King Dryga said. "Even the serpents failed in their occupation. King Blu would need the power of all the ocean to prevail."

There was quiet for a moment as both lords thought the unspoken: King Blu might have that power–and more.

"The eagles have returned, new king of *Animus Nor*," Sky Death said. "They say that there are no portals for a three suns' journey in any direction."

"Perhaps the whale god no longer needs portals," Pale Ghost said.

The ancient rodent, still unearthly in his hue, was blinded by seeing too many seasons of sun and war. Yet, his great-grandchild, Silent Wind, had some of his great-grandfather in the fire that sparked the purple of his eyes.

"That doesn't mean we don't," Silent Wind said. "You once told me, great-grandfather, in the legends of The Serpent War, that Sky Death and Moon Shadow once created an illusion: a mystical flight of eagles that allowed for escape. Perhaps we should create an illusion: a web of portals, below the mountains. King Blu might send his best troops to dismantle them. We could then attack and have the advantage."

"Clever mouse," Pale Ghost said. "If only there were somewhere left to run."

"Still, the idea is a worthy one," King Dryga said. "Build your decoy. We can use every delay that we can get."

"Yet, that will not be enough," Shadow Dancer, the other great-grandchild of Pale Ghost, said. "We have one fundamental advantage: We are on land, yet The Army of The Black Ocean needs water to fight. If we can take away any water, evaporate it, we can hold the forces of King Blu at bay."

"And just how do you propose to do that?" Pale Ghost asked.

"Orij spoke of the dragon emperor's use of a fire shield to buffer the armies of the ocean before they could strike," Shadow Dancer said. "The wily dragon had a sound strategy–only, the shield was not powerful enough. We need to amplify it so that it evaporates water and extend it to the heart of *Gungsung Dor* itself."

"Not with a million mice could we accomplish that in time," Pale Ghost said. "Besides, the dragons are lost to the sea. How can we accomplish this without their fire?"

"Lightning," Shadow Dancer said. "If we can harness the power of the sky, we can use King Blu's own magic against him."

"Do so," King Dryga said. "If we can make this magic work for us, we can send spies to any animal kingdoms that are left. They, too, might be saved."

The mice scurried off, arguing over which plan had greater merit. King Dryga stayed with Igru as Dasu, the great cat queen, came forward.

"How far away is the ocean now? Do the cats or eagles know?" King Dryga asked.

Sky Death and Dasu looked at each other.

"Within three suns," Sky Death said.

"Sooner," Dasu spoke. "King Blu has used the power of The Great Northern Waters against us. All the greatest lakes now swirl with storms, helping the ocean to expand inward."

"And how many were lost?" King Dryga inquired.

"Untold thousands," Dasu said, "who could not migrate in time or get far enough away from the advancing storms."

"There is still more, my lord," Sky Death said.

"Yes?" King Dryga asked.

"The Night Eye, the treacherous flock that sought the highest of thrones in The Serpent War, are back," Sky Death said. "They appear as if resurrected from the dead. They are the eyes of King Blu in the air, and they are at the head of the storms that signal the coming of the whale god. Wherever they go, death follows."

"Then they shall be the first to fall," King Dryga said.

King Dryga looked over at Ice Giant, who looked back with old, uncertain eyes.

"Get the animals to the mountain caves–as many as can fit," King Dryga said. "Have The Blood Paw split up, guarding both the caves and the edge of the mountains. They are to attack whatever the whale god first sends our way."

"Yes, my lord," Ice Giant said.

"And what shall we do, my lord?" Igru asked.

"Let all surviving animal lords comfort their tribes," King Dryga replied. "There is still some hope. I can still hear the words of Freyda in my ear."

The animals headed off, hoping that the fate of their tribes depended upon more than a fleeting whim of salvation.

"Fewer than three suns remain," King Dryga said to the storm-filled skies. "Let us hope that even gods can fall."

Ulindu

Yukon River, Alaska, USA

Silver Snake, once a forgotten otter king, thought back to the time before time as the storm waters came upon him. Long ago, he had warned the first animal council that he feared where this was all leading. Now, generations removed, the ancient king who served but fleetingly in two wars saw how wrong the animal lords had gotten it. The feeble otter, unable to outswim the legions of Admiral Xrata, awaited Death. Yet, to the venerable old soul, Death was not the fearsome gaze of the whale god. To Silver Snake, Death was a playful, magic otter who had finally caught up with him after a game of hiding behind phantom brush that got caught in the river of Time. Occasionally, Silver Snake would lift his head from the river waters to see if he gave his old friend the slip. Yet, the garrulous otter was still there, still hunting, still chattering on about what he'd seen over so many years, just a few currents away. Once, generations ago, Silver Snake thought of what the end of his days might entail. He thought of being surrounded by an enormous family of otters swimming free of the pointless destruction of the *rulku*. Yet, here he was, the victim of another pointless war. Earth is a river, Silver Snake thought, playful and free. The birds once flew without need of conquest. The bears roamed while sharing the same woodlands with the mountain lion and bobcat. Even the wolves and coyotes coexisted, whatever friction may have formed between Crimson Fang and Moon Shadow, two names lost in the River of Time. What changed–and why?

Looking out as he circled in the river one last time, Silver Snake pitied the one who sent the storm bent on consuming even the most pristine rivers of *Animus Nor.* However much the conquerors' names would be used to scare the little baby otters of the future into staying at their mothers' sides, what did the great conquerors of the animal world–the Azazes, Thraxises, and King Blus–really know of life? Taking in the last morsel of the sun as the fox sparrows flew off, with its dipping icy reds, pinks, and golds, Silver Snake saw the true treasure. If only the animal world would understand. True treasure is a half-set sun, on a golden river, the moment spring breaks. True treasure is the circling sky the moment baby otters cry out in joy in their first breaths of life. Nothing else compares. The River of Time comes for all, anyway. Why not go out with a laugh rather than with a cry? And so, one last time, Silver Snake chased the sun, his leaping laughter the only sound of true life upon the vanquishing waters.

CHAPTER 10

Klang Uktor
Congo, Africa

In the jungle mists, at the grassland palace of Yanta, Klang Krugal and Sun Stalker listened. Qwizly, the black-browed albatross, spoke in the old *Osine* of the fortifications he had seen at *Gola Dwyn* and of the spies he had sent by the waters of *Seerus-Ungalore*.

"As it is, my lords," Qwizly said, "*Seerus-Ungalore* will not survive. One large tsunami is all that's needed for King Blu to wipe its highest fortifications from the earth. Fire Hoof, the reindeer king, has brought all animal tribes to the continent. The Night Eye, a massive flock now split between all continents, rule for King Blu. In *Seerus-Ungalore,* they still use the perch of the old *rulku* Tower as their own."

"And what of *Gola Dwyn*?" Klang Krugal asked.

"The snakes put much stock in the prophecies of Thraxis, the fallen empress," Qwizly said. "They believe that, through her, they have an eye into the plans of the whale god. Xyla and her boas plan to use their magic to turn saltwater fresh, in the hopes of slowing the advance of The Army of The Black Ocean. *Gola Dwyn* may prove the hardest land to take."

"That leaves *Animus Nor,*" Yanta said, "once a beacon of hope to the animal world."

Qwizly collected his words carefully before bluntly saying, "*Animus Nor* is a lost kingdom, according to my spies. King Dryga wisely pulls all animal tribes to the highest peaks of *Gungsung Dor*, but the whale god will make it his personal quest to make sure that the holy place where animals first stood against *rulku* falls swiftly. Like *Yvot-Sing* and its legion of dragons, *Animus Nor* will receive the personal presence of the whale god. I don't know how they can survive."

Qwizly took another breath before adding, "However, the animal tribes there have foreseen their own doom. They sent the hawk lord, Death Talon, to deliver a message. They have a weapon to face The Army of The Black Ocean, one they wish to share with us."

Sun Stalker asked, "What weapon can overcome a god?"

"Ingenuity," Qwizly answered. "They propose a giant shield powered by lightning and a personal force field that evaporates the water the sharks need to hunt."

"That sounds promising," Yanta said. "Send this intel to the elephant Stampeders, the ape lords, and the Sun Pride at once, so that all may put this weapon to use."

"Yes, elephant queen," Qwizly said, fluttering his mighty wings. He turned his taciturn eye on the animal lords and said, "There is one more thing you should know before I fly off. The *rulku* boy Thraxis kept as her personal pet is now a viper, fully grown. Aeyra killed Groth The Impaler and seeks to kill all the original animal lords. Your father is not safe."

"The *rulku* are crafty killers, with little regard for what is *Ozu*," Yanta said. "Yet, I'd like to see the *rulku* abomination stand against my Stampeders."

"My messages are delivered," Qwizly said. "What you do with them is up to you, my lords."

With that, Qwizly flew off, joining a massive fluttering of messenger birds sweeping the sky. So many birds flew back and forth that the entire jungle was abuzz with the news of King Blu's conquests. Earl The Equivocator translated between the kingdoms of the newly advanced, still lacking in the common language. All the greater and lesser flamingos could buzz about was the arrival of a strange murder of crows, neither alive nor dead, from *Seerus-Ungalore*."

"Can The Night Eye be on our shores already?" Yanta asked the other lords. "Truly, the messenger is right. I thought The Night Eye ruled as puppet queens in *Yvot-Sing*. Shall we send any birds out to meet them?"

"I say one of us parlays with the birds of destiny," Sun Stalker said. "I shall go."

"Your bravery does you credit, lion lord," Klang Krugal said. "But now is the time for caution. Let us bring the birds to the jungles to share their messages of doom. They wouldn't dare assassinate us with the whole jungle ready to pounce."

"Agreed," Yanta said. "My elephants shall stand guard."

"As will my apes," Klang Krugal said.

"And my lions, leopards, and wildcats," Sun Stalker said.

"Let them assemble by The Golden Temple Of *Avrah*," Klang Krugal said. "Let the eyes of King Blu look upon those of a true god."

Yanta trumpeted her approval. Sun Stalker roared his. The animal lords of the jungle and savannah called Earl The Equivocator.

"Great parrot king," Klang Krugal said. "Can you fly the birds of fortune to us?"

"I will deliver your message in all the languages of the known animal world," Earl said.

"If The Night Eye wish to talk, they will come. If they wish to fight, you will find out soon enough."

"If you allow it, leave one of your nanobots here to project what you say and do," Yanta said. "We will summon the hawks and eagles of the region to attack at the first moment of danger."

With that, the great parrot king flew farther than most parrots fly in a lifetime, towards the greater coasts where Thraxis The Conqueror once invaded. The marks that her massive fire body burned into the rock still glowed at evening time. Still, Earl did not need to fly far before he saw a large host of birds, their eyes sundry colors trapped in deathly white. In them, Earl saw a world of fire and destruction. The birds themselves had stiff feathers that looked more unearthly than animal. It was as if The Great Sun that gave life had burned them into death, yet they flew at the brink of both worlds, neither alive nor dead.

"Where are the animal lords now," Mother Raven asked, "who once spoke with such fury and such thunder? Is The Oracle Of The Whale God enough to scare them away so soon?

As if in a Greek chorus, another raven spoke, adding, "If so, the animal lords are wiser than we thought. Yet, what is wisdom in the face of the eternal one, King Blu?"

"I am only the messenger of the lords," Earl the Equivocator said. "To my birds, you are as the *rulku–avitan,* unholy, accursed traitors of your kind. Follow me, if you can fly without stabbing a bird's back feathers with your forked beaks. The animal lords will soon give you their answer."

The Night Eye cackled. "Such fire will be gone when death comes over you, parrot puppet king," the host of The Night Eye said as one. "If your lords try to trap us, the one who sees all will leave no jungle animal alive."

Earl the Equivocator gave a hissing cackle of his own before flying off. The Night Eye followed, large enough to blot out the sun as they moved from coast to savannah to the heart of the jungle. Mother Raven cackled when she saw the grand temple built in the image of the sun.

"The fabled Golden Temple Of *Avrah,*" The Night Eye said. "And who sits at the feet of the temple but the animal lords themselves? What a message! You will soon see whether even the power of the mighty mirror goddess can withstand King Blu's destruction."

The face of *Avrah*, a half-eclipsed sun, gazed up from the temple, as if anxious to reply. Sun Stalker skulked about the birds that fluttered in endless unison. Klang Krugal observed blankly, as if overwhelmed by the sight. Yanta turned her old eyes upon The Night Eye, half in pity, half in terror.

"So, this is what became of the would-be empress birds?" Yanta asked rhetorically. "Once so mighty. Now, effigies of fallen glory. Well, tell your god this, servant birds: as long as *Avrah* lives, we live as well."

The Night Eye fluttered more quietly, their inquisitive nature overcoming their hubris. Mother Raven looked into the eyes of the elephant queen and saw no lie.

"*Avrah* will not save you," The Night Eye prophesied. "Against the tidal wave of the divine, there is no survival."

"And yet, here you are," Klang Krugal said. "Surely, the whale god did not send you only to prophesy our doom. Get to the point, equivocating ravens. What is it that you want?"

"Or rather," Sun Stalker asked, "what is it that you fear?"

The Night Eye fluttered, cackling dismissively. "When Death reaches out and clutches your throat, you'll be amazed at how quickly fear turns to numbness," Mother Raven said. "We fear nothing. You fear much. We are here to offer you terms of surrender: no more, no less."

"Then speak," Yanta said. "The seabirds say the whale god takes no prisoners."

"Seabirds never lie," The Night Eye said. "Gather all of your kind upon the great southern shore. There, the whale god will visit you in his mercy, and you shall not suffer. Ignore this decree, and you will suffer much before the flame of vitality flickers and is no more."

"Is that how you died?" Yanta asked.

"We are *nvrhyth,* alive some moments, dead at others, depending on the pleasure of King Blu," The Night Eye said. "So, do you accept the whale god's terms or not?"

The animal lords looked at each other, but Klang Krugal, still with a touch of the temper of old, spoke first.

"We do not," Klang Krugal said, plainly. "We, in turn, offer terms of surrender from the great *Avrah* above, defender of all animals. Tell King Blu to leave our shores immediately with all of his legions. If not, the light of *Avrah* will vanquish the darkness of the whale god as the sun vanquishes the moon. The whale god may prevail over us, but not over *Avrah*, and not before many of his children of the sea perish."

"We shall see," The Night Eye said, one crow after another, "which god holds more power over *Klang Uktor*."

The Night Eye fluttered in a massive circle, flying ever upward, as if to obliterate the sun. Just as suddenly, they were gone, at once there and vanished, no more than shadows lining the pale edge of an even paler cloud. The animal lords looked out to see the ocean rising, frothing with the sky. Against the endless shadow of light, a single set of wet, broken wings emerged.

"Qwizly?" Yanta asked, trying to make out the full shape of the bird.

"Quickly, lords," Qwizly said. "The Stampeders have a message. The great mice lords reached out with a weapon that may yet dim the tides of the whale god's fortunes."

Yanta trumpeted the alarm. Sun Stalker added his most ferocious growl. Even the ape lord cried out in anguished warning. Heaven and earth and the animals that inhabited them moved, as if *Avrah* herself awoke from the earth's bosom. Behind the fleeing animals rose a gigantic wave, crashing into the earth, filled with great white sharks and giant squids. And so, the wrath of King Blu was upon them.

Gungsung Dor

Bear Mountain, Rockies, USA

Pale Thunder and the eagles, Death Talon and the hawks, and Sky Death and the buzzards circled around in such a tizzy that they looked like the black cloud of the undead Night Eye themselves.

"One at a time," King Dryga ordered. "In *Osine*."

"Great king of *Animus Nor*," Sky Death said, as if speaking to Azaz of old, "King Blu has struck all the remaining lands at once. Fire Hoof evacuated *Seerus-Ungalore* just before the massive tsunamis struck. One wall of water after another submerged the land so that The Tower of The Night Eye is one of the few structures partially above water. Fire Hoof holds the icy lands, hoping that ice might slow the onslaught of the whale god."

"*Klang Uktor* fares little better," Pale Thunder said. "Colossal tides and storms like the animal kingdom has never seen move inland. The jungle lords brace for the worst of it. Our spies tell us that The Army of The Black Ocean is nearly at their shores."

"Have you contacted the animal lords about your weapon?" King Dryga asked.

"My mice's transmissions went unanswered," Pale Ghost said. "I dare not put the plans into the nanosphere, lest King Blu's spies hear all that we say. Death Talon flew instead."

"I flew in stealth," Death Talon said. "The Night Eye had already arrived, perhaps to stake out their claim. I could not speak with Earl the Equivocator. Instead, Qwizly, the albatross lord, spoke with me. He relayed the message. We shall see if the ape lords and Stampeders are up to the task."

"Any word from Methuselah or Queen Diurnia?" King Dryga asked.

"The ancient language of the trees is tough to interpret in *Osine*," Sky Death said. "But the gist of their message is that they will strike soon, when the time is right."

"Not exactly reassuring," King Dryga said. "But then again, a witch's answers seldom are."

"Nonetheless, the great tree queens may prove as valuable as they did in The *Rulku* War, if your higher spirit, Azaz, does not mind my saying so," Sky Death added.

"Azaz does mind," King Dryga said, "but I do not. What of Fire Hoof?" King Dryga asked, turning to Ice Giant.

"My polar bears delivered the plans from one to another, until we thought it safe," Ice Giant said, looking towards Igru, lord of the musk oxen. "We then passed it off to Igru's spies."

"One of my oxen spoke with the reindeer king," Igru said. "Fire Hoof feared we came too late, but he turned to an unlikely ally: The Rat King. The king led a group of *rulku*-hunting rats from *Yvot-Sing* before the great flood. He tinkers with the plans now."

"Honor among rats," Sky Death said. "Now, I have seen everything."

"Not everything," a familiar voice, half-snarl, half-growl, called out.

The animal lords turned to see Dasu, the great cat, leading Freyda the Fatal and an entourage consisting of Moon Herald, Snow Prophet, and Criddock The Cudgel, in the flesh. The young wolf lord looked lean and hungry from many nights of running. The owl looked weathered, with strident wings. The tortoise looked rather plump, as if from a remarkably short journey. Yet, all eyes were on the great bear queen mother, who looked leaner, but nastier than ever, with eyes as white and storm-filled as those of The Night Eye themselves.

"Mother," King Dryga said, not without gentleness. "Can it be?'

"The king of *Animus Nor*," Freyda said, with a snarl. "You have need of your mother now, don't you? You all have need of Mother Witch now."

"The witches traveled far, my lord," Dasu said. "I figured they'd pose no harm now, at the last hour."

King Dryga shook his crownless head. "A witch is always at her most dangerous when she's hunting," he said. "But it is no matter, Dasu. I'd rather have you here, Mother Bear, at the end of the animal age, to fight together one last time against our father's murderer."

A great growl shook the skies. The spirit of Azaz hovered over the dispossessed king yet.

"I sense Azaz," Freyda said, "but your father would never speak in fear. There is always a way, my son, even when you come face to face with Death himself."

Moon Herald limped behind Freyda, half-beaten by his run. Snow Prophet sat perched among the eagles, letting the witch have her due. And Criddock stood there, every so often opening his turtle jaw as if to interject, but stopping short of words, which was probably for the best. The animal lords all turned to Freyda, waiting for whatever incantation might come next.

"There is no one spell, no red nanobot, no mighty crown that will set the animal world free of the wrath of King Blu," Freyda said, pacing around. "Rather, the spirit body of *Avrah* must be restored."

"Do you not know the legends?" Sky Death asked. "*Avrah* chose not to be incarnated, unlike the whale god."

"And how does that legend end, wise old bird?" Freyda asked.

Sky Death said, simply, "*Then the sea shall swallow them, and we shall start anew,* King Blu said. *For no creature is above Avrah, and no creature is above King Blu.*"

"Exactly the propaganda the whale god would have you believe," Freyda said. "I have learned much studying with the trees in my exile. The true legend is more complicated. *Ozu-Ry*, the creator god, wanted to experience Creation. And so, *Ozu-Ry* reincarnated itself, male and female, into *Avrah* and King Blu. *Avrah* controlled the lands and the birds of the sky. King Blu controlled the ocean, its creatures, and any birds that flew over the sea. When they fought to form the perfect creation, King Blu formed the sponges and the whales and all the creatures of the sea. *Avrah* formed the creatures of the land. Until King Blu sent the spirit of death into one of these creatures who rode his waters without permission, the *rulku*. They hunted the land creatures nearly to extinction and poisoned the seas. Still, King Blu waited until the perfect time for them to spread their nanobots to the world, to awaken the other animals who would kill the *rulku* in revenge for the loss of life on the seas. Yet, *Avrah* had different ideas. She split her sacred body again, reincarnating as the spirit of the wolf, of the bear, of the eagle, of the *rulku*, of the ape, of the elephant, of the giant panda, of all the original animal lords. King Blu sensed her energy and thus saved the last of the *rulku* at the end of the first great war. However, the animals have since angered him. Their deaths–and the living breath of her oracle–will bring *Avrah's* body together for one last fight against her apocalyptic mirror god."

"And how can you say for sure?" Sky Death asked.

Freyda smirked. "Look to the power of Azaz, even now, or to the visions of the great white wolf who runs with The Fire Wolf," she said. "They are all *Avrah* fighting to come back before it is too late. Even the great whale god cannot overcome the full power of *Avrah*. Like two opposing forces, they will vanquish one another, and the storms will grow still."

Snow Prophet flapped his wings, saying, "The songs of Creation must be sung in answer to the great whale songs of the sea. Only a powerful witch can sing the song while the spirits of *Avrah* come together for one last fight. And only in the cradle of *Avrah*, in the heart of the land, can this song be sung."

"Tell me, Oracle of the North," Sky Death said. "What will become of these original animal lords?"

"They must perish for *Avrah* to be reborn," Snow Prophet declared.

"Even me?" Sky Death asked.

"I'm sorry, my friend," Snow Prophet said. "There are some things not even a seer can see. All our fates hang in the hands of *Avrah* now."

"Then what must we do?" King Dryga asked.

"King Blu will stop our union at all costs," Snow Prophet said. "He hides the dragon lord, the connection to the holy great panda, from us. We must face the wrath of the whale god and fare better than *Yvot-Sing* or *Seerus-Ungalore*. Only then can we come together on the last spot of unflooded earth to face the whale god. In the meantime, Wylaka, the great orca hunter, has been sighted along the coasts. Qylar The Hunter also circles around, seeing if he can disable our offenses. We must bring down the commanders of King Blu–and flee before the whale god himself breaches."

The animal lords all looked upon each other, turning to the high king of *Animus*.

"So be it," King Dryga said. "Let the Blood Paw, Igru and his legions, and even the mighty snakes, surround the mountain. The time to draw blood has come."

King Dryga let up a great summoning cry, and the fire of Azaz burned upon his fangs.

CHAPTER 11

Seerus-Ungalore
London, England

At least one-third of The Night Eye remained in *Seerus-Ungalore* to oversee the transition from rock to ocean. Massive migrations of birds, all with news from the various kingdoms, came to The Tower, one of the few standing structures, to report the progress of King Blu's campaign. Still, few animals still roamed the forlorn island that once dominated the *rulku* world. Even fewer bodies, mainly unawakened moles, sewer rats, red foxes who had outwitted the animal kingdom for the last time, flowed down the river before being devoured by sharks. Still, The Night Eye knew that in silence was danger. Fire Hoof had evacuated and given up the crown jewel of his kingdom too easily. Wayward ravens reported that the golden-antlered reindeer king bunkered in the northern Alps, readying to fight with ice and rock by his side. Yet, The Night Eye knew: animals don't leave their hunting grounds so easily.

That's when the ever-roaming eye of one cagey crow caught the sight. A starry smooth-hound shark feeding greedily upon the body of a fallen, unawakened bear cub coughed out its own blood. A gray-blue northern bottlenose whale, straying from its usual diet of sea cucumbers, sampled a dead albino rat and paid the price. It too coughed up blood, but an unnatural bloody phlegm, filled with green nanobots that looked predatory in nature.

Crows cackled, and ravens swarmed. The Night Eye realized their folly. The half-consumed bodies of dead foxes were strewn with deep, hunter green mosses and liverworts, and liverworts are nothing if not spiteful. The few awakened plants the ravens had encountered in their travels had constantly warned any encroaching birds about landing upon their children. And now, here was the great king of the sea, sending a plague upon the plant world to kill off the animals that depended upon them. Somehow, some way, The Night Eye knew,

King Blu had made a fatal error. The plant witch Methuselah and her sisters had laid a trap. The underwater world now had its foot caught in the snare.

"Cease in your feasting," The Night Eye cried out in cacophonous clamor. "Eat and die! The plant witch mother, Methuselah, has struck! The animals are loaded with parasitic nanobots, King Blu," The Night Eye said in summons. There was nothing more to say. If they knew, King Blu knew as well. The conniving crows looked through the white eyes of their brothers and sisters from *Klang Uktor* to *Animus Sur* and *Animus Nor.* Elsewhere, it was the same. Methuselah had released a plague upon the plague maker, and there was no telling how much its mighty jaws might devour.

From deep in the bowels of the sea, the waves shook in fearsome reply. The whale song was so intricate and so thunderous, even the birds shook in the skies.

"Fall back, my children," the mouth of King Blu called out through The Night Eye. "Let the tsunamis do your work for you. Come back to the sea—to healing, to shelter."

The whales, dolphins, and sharks retreated to the arms of their divine father.

Yet, all was not well with *Seerus-Ungalore.* The tsunamis, with a water-shifting nebulous body, arose. As King Blu's fourth great plague, they struck down the mountains, hills, and valleys. In a matter of moments, *Seerus-Ungalore* was no more.

$$\approx$$

Yyve-Tolten

The Northern Shores
Nunavut, Canada

The frozen wave, a whiplike archipelago of ice, storm, and sea, crashed. Its spiked tail brought not only half-melted glacial ice but the first of Wylaka's soldiers. Trained killers, the orcas waited until the waves knocked the polar bears over the slickening edge of land. The moment a paw or snout submerged, Wylaka's whales were there to tear the bear to pieces.

A second wave rose, icier and taller than the last.

"Hold firm," Ice Giant ordered, watching the wave and the whales. "Hold together."

After all of Pale Ghost's ceaseless labor, after Silent Wind and Shadow Dancer's endless tinkering, this was the moment of truth. The heated energy field would be either the last blow or the last line of defense. Polar bears waited to see if they would succumb to the wrath of the whale god. The wave struck. Ice shattered. Whales lunged. Heat burned the waters until only the hardness of prehistoric ice remained. Two of Wylaka's whales lay prone on the ice, crying out for their brothers.

"Now," Ice Giant commanded. "Show the whale god the meaning of death!"

Ice Giant's best polar bears lunged, tearing greedily at the orca tribes until the massive whales lost head and fin to the onslaught. Wylaka looked on, perplexed, searching out any vulnerable areas in the ice. The bears were just as quick, pulling two of the smaller orcas towards the water-burning energy field. The burn seared the whales. One broke off, scalded and scarred, in retreat. The other orca felt the full wrath of the bears.

The whales whistled, clicked, and called over the waters. Ice Giant may not have known the language, but he knew its meaning. The whales swam the perimeter, feeling out where the shield might be.

The polar bears struck with the full fury of nature. They reached into the ice, scratching and clawing at the orcas as the whales passed. The orcas lunged for the ice, throwing their total weight against the shield of fire that separated them from Ice Giant's lieutenants. Still, the orcas could not break through the shield.

From above the ice, Sky Death circled. The orcas looked up. They whistled amongst their pod, uncertain whether the big black bird of death was one of the dreaded Night Eye or another entity altogether.

"What is it?" Ice Giant asked as Sky Death descended upon the ice.

"News from the king of *Animus Nor*," Sky Death said. "The tree witch Methuselah has reached out to us after all. A strange plague overtakes the sea beast of *Seerus-Ungalore*. The Army of The Black Ocean succeeded in taking the seat of power, but at considerable cost."

"I would trade a paw to have that plague now," Ice Giant said, as the whales mounted a fresh offense against the fire shield. "Our defenses cannot hold forever."

"They will not have to," Sky Death said. "King Dryga has other plans."

The wise old turkey vulture looked at the sky, in all its frozen pinks and reds, just before another volley of ice and snow took them over.

"I was never a fighter," Sky Death said. "I would rather welcome Death by a warm fire, in a grand feast for the ages. But who truly knows the mind of Death? It comes when it comes. All we can do is take the hand of *Avrah* and trust that she guides us to a new, gentler sun. That is why, today, I welcome the death of a warrior bird. May Thunder Killer welcome me to The Great Nesting Ground the way we once bid Moon Shadow farewell in The Great Hunt. If I survive the initial volley, send a bear after me. If not, I thank whatever ancestor birds there may be for the glory of a fresh kill, for the ecstasy of a flight in favorable winds, for the sacred breath I first breathed, long before the *rulku* unleashed their magic against us. That was life."

Sky Death flew off, right through the perimeter, green nanobots crawling up from his old, jaded feathers. The orca lunged up at him. Just as Wylaka grabbed at Sky Death's right wing with his gargantuan whale jaws, the green nanobots descended.

"Get to the edge of the ice," Ice Giant ordered. "Save that noble vulture at all costs!"

Wylaka spit out the bird the moment the nanobots overtook his massive jaw. The nanobots burrowed their way into Wylaka's rich, dense orca skin. Green nanobots multiplied, digging into even the great whale hunter's eyes. The orca king hissed and whistled, shaking the nanobots from him. Fresh nanobots appeared, digging deeper. The orca troops backed off, fleeing their once formidable commander. Yet, the flight was too late. The green nanobots leapt from orca to orca, burrowing and poisoning them. The orcas splashed around in the great northern waters.

"Retreat," Wylaka said. "Save yourselves, my brothers and sisters."

The orcas surrounded their leader, crying out in elegy.

"Let me die so that you might live," Wylaka commanded. "Swim off, far from this place, before the plague jumps to you. It was a joy to hunt with you. Now, swim!"

A huge whale song, shattering the rest of the noise, stirred the orcas. The orcas fled, clicking and crying. Wylaka and the other infected members of the pod writhed, shaking, biting at the nanobots, but it was no use. Wylaka swam his last battle. The nanobots consumed him before heading to fresh waters. Wylaka's whale carcass breached the waters before falling, still and half-eaten, to the ocean ice below.

The polar bears brought the dying bird back to the ice. Sky Death, the old, cantankerous bird that he was, clung to his last breaths feverishly. He would not die alone after all. The great celebration of bears honored his sacrifice with a growl that rattled the ice itself. Against the wet, ice-strewn odds, the land animals had won a victory, if only for a moment.

Just then, Ice Giant looked out and saw the storm clouds circling. The ocean became a whirlpool as the waves grew impossibly larger. Sea and sky surged until no bear could tell where one ended and the other began. An impossibly gigantic body, half-blue, half-black, with markings along its sides, breached the waters.

"Fall back," Ice Giant ordered, lifting Sky Death's body upon his back. "Do not look the whale god in the eyes! Flee to the higher rock! Fall back to The Blood Paw! I will keep the dying vulture safe!"

The bears joined the other land fauna in a massive flight, retreating from the ice.

There was another whale cry, this one loud enough to shake even the earth itself.

King Blu was upon them.

CHAPTER 12

Gola Dwyn, Animus Sur

The Amazon Rainforest

Xyla's legion of red snakes soared from the ocean like a tower of slithering might. Even Qylar The Hunter, the giant octopus intelligence operative, couldn't find a way past the outer rim of the mythical *Gola Dwyn,* the Atlantis of the southern seas. Xrata's second legion remained, even as the great white shark admiral swam thousands of miles away, preparing for the next assault on *Klang Uktor.* In his place, the whale god summoned King Croc, whose legions of half-*rulku,* half crocodilian monstrosities readied themselves for a prolonged fight.

Xyla, the mother boa, wrapped her body around The Throne Tower trees. The Golden Eye of *Gola Dwyn* still shone, shards of the mighty crown Thraxis The Terrible once wore. The jungle beneath was still golden, still full of towering river tree trunks and militias of snake, caiman, and experimental terror lizards, ready for the fight. The architecture consisted of less laboratories and more glistening battle towers, filled with unholy magic of all kinds. Flying machines still hovered, with *rulku* magic not seen since the days of Azaz. And around them all, the few great *allosaurus* beasts that did not die in The Serpent War. Beneath the river, peppering the majestic Amazon, were further terror lizards, such as the *sarcosuchus imperator* and the mosasaurus hybrids of the last great war.

By Xyla's side stood the laughing goddess, madly staring ahead at the calculating ocean lords. She still bore an albino fire upon her black-green skin, a creature caught between worlds, like The Night Eye before her.

"I have seen the eyes of the whale god," Thraxis called. "He sees all. Covets all. Thinks that all is his. But still his primordial eyes search, endlessly, for his twin goddess. The spark of *Avrah* lives, and King Blu feels the fire."

Xyla motioned to her viper guards to take the insane ex-empress to her room. Yet, a preternatural power held Thraxis in place.

"Wipe the earth clean, whale god," Thraxis called, "and still, you will not find her. While one lives, the other dies; when one dies, the other is reborn. As the moon sets and the sun rises, and the sun sets and the moon rises, so will it be until The Vanquishing. The whale god sees this. He fears it above all else. Yet, it is as certain as the ebbing tide."

"But what of the whale god's plan?" Xyla asked her mad empress. "What of *Gola Dwyn?*"

"*Gola Dwyn* shall pay the full price of the whale god's wrath," Thraxis said. "If she is to live, it will be by the blood of the *rulku*, by the very magic of *Avrah*."

Xyla stared, her serpentine face half-frozen in wonder and confusion.

Seconds later, the monstrous crocodile king, all scales and scars, stepped forward. His yellow eyes rested upon The Throne Tower and the sparkling white fire of the shattered crown.

"I am the voice of the whale god," King Croc said. "I am chosen to speak to the fallen lords of *Gola Dwyn* the great whale song in the *Osine* language, so that all will hear. Listen to the message recorded by my lord."

King Croc nodded, and Qylar the Hunter summoned a holographic transmission from depths of the sea no landling had ever charted. The song itself was thunder, shaking the tower and rustling the waters into cyclones that spun and hurled. King Croc waited until the transmission ended before offering his own words.

"King Blu, the rightful high king of all high kings and lord of all life," King Croc said, "has pronounced a sentence upon you and your kingdom. *Gola Dwyn*, the whale god decrees, had the potential to be the brightest of suns to a primordially dark world. Instead, the energy of a broken crown sits in its highest tower, a reminder of its own failures. You, brothers and sisters, are creatures adapted to the sea. If you do as *Ku-Rah* did, if you turn over all *rulku* and anaconda magic to King Blu's forces, you will be allowed to live in the sea as the brothers and sisters that you were meant to be. However, if you refuse my lord's most gracious offer, if you continue in this blasphemy, you will suffer the fate of your kingdom. Like the Atlantis of the *rulku* world, your mighty river civilization shall fall to the waters of devastation, and you will die, eaten by sharks and monsters. You have one sunrise to decide."

Xyla looked at Vesper The Red, who in turn looked at Thraxis.

"Their numbers," Vesper said, "are far too great for our forces. Either way, the kingdom of *Gola Dwyn* will be lost, as *Seerus-Ungalore, Yvot Sing,* and *Animus Nor* before it."

"To turn over our technology to the whale god is to commit euthanasia," Xyla said. "I would rather destroy a generation's worth of experimentation than allow King Blu to use it to eradicate our brothers and sisters of the land. They, too, are my subjects."

"The vipers will fight to the death if you command it," Vesper replied. "What are your orders, my empress?"

Xyla weighed the matter.

"You were a faithful servant," Thraxis said to Xyla, "but you never truly thought like a snake."

"Silence," Xyla said. "Your provocations led to this. Let me think."

Thraxis laughed. "Can you blame a snake for strangling the life out of an animal that might serve as its greatest lunch?" she asked. "Foolish queen, I was but the harbinger, a puppet queen, as you are, before the lord of the sea waged his horrible war. But I thought like a snake then, and I think like a snake still. You're not cold-blooded enough to be my successor, so listen to me now. Make peace. Allow the sea generals into the city. Let the armies of the ocean divide themselves and spread out over the expanse of the Amazon. And then, when the moment is right, squeeze the life out of every commander King Blu sends our way. Such is the way of the snake."

"And then what?" Xyla asked. "Our snakes will be slaughtered, our kingdom lost. There are simply too many crocodiles, terror lizards, and sharks."

"There's a plague for everything, even the forces of King Blu," Thraxis said with a laugh. "The witch tree, Methuselah, knows that. Why don't you?"

"King Blu was right about one thing," Xyla said, looking at the fallen empress. "We have become monstrosities, poisoning ourselves like the *rulku* before us."

"Eat or be eaten, child," Thraxis said. "It's the only way."

Xyla slithered all throughout The Throne Room, if only to get away from the poisonous shadow of her former empress. She thought back to the plans she had after Thraxis' dramatic demise. Empress Xyla would be the Snake Queen of Life, the one who used the magic of the riverbeds of *Gola Dwyn* to make the lives of the fabled kingdom better than any animal life in all of history had ever been. She would breed a generation of magicians and thinkers who might heal the wounds of war, who might create the most prosperous kingdom the animal world had ever seen. But now, whether well-intentioned or vainglorious, such dreams were folly. Thraxis was right. Xyla thought of the irony of that for just a moment: a snake maddened by war was right. What had the world come to? If only King Blu had been honorable. If only it were a time of peace. But in war, madness and reason are one and the same. After hours of slithering well into the night, Xyla emerged from her seclusion.

A messenger boa constrictor, Mandau, bowed her head before the queen.

"What news?" Xyla asked, half-listening.

"*Animus Nor* is quiet," Mandau said. "King Dryga lives upon the highest peak, surrounded by water. The army of the polar bear king prevailed, killing Wylaka and spreading contagion to the seas. The old sage Sky Death may have been mortally wounded spreading the nanovirus. Countless other bear, wolf, and deer bodies line the waters. Now, the whale god himself has been spotted, heading straight for *Yyve-Tolten.* The buzz in the ocean waters is that King Blu will use his power of the storm to flood *Animus Nor* all the way to *Gungsung Dor.* He means to challenge King Dryga himself."

"So, *Animus Nor* has already played our hand and lost," Xyla said. "Thraxis is right. Send word to King Croc. Tell him we agree to surrender, provided all animals of *Gola Dwyn* are seen as subjects of King Blu, under his holy protection."

"Are you sure, my queen?" Mandau asked.

"When even peace is war and war is peace, who can be sure of anything?" Xyla replied.

Mandau plunged back into the night waters. Xyla slithered towards the great white fire above The Throne Tower. The broken crown still sparkled, still burned in perennial flame. Xyla shook her head, hissed, and slithered away.

Klang Uktor

Congo, Africa

"Here it comes," Klang Krugal called from the seat of *Avrah.*

The massive cyclone of water, wind, and lightning smashed everything in front of it. Even without the pillar portals, King Blu was indeed mighty. Over the past several moon cycles, the whale god had pushed the sea to the jungle. Now, the bunkered land animals saw the fruit of the god's labors: a cyclone so massive not even the distant jungles were spared.

Yanta and her Stampeders formed a perimeter around the towering statue of *Avrah*, as the apes swung from the foundation stones. Sun Stalker and the lions crouched, preparing to pounce, as did the cheetahs and leopards, who snarled at the advancing wave. Earl the Equivocator, Qwizly, and half the bird kingdom surveyed the air, shouting updates to the land animals from the skies.

"The giant squids lead the charge," Earl said. "Yet, the sharks are the true weapons. Prepare yourselves. Xrata and the great white sharks come in directly after the squids ensnare you with their tentacles."

"Let's hope the magic of the mice lords is as powerful as they say," Yanta replied. "My Stampeders will crush the squids. Klang Krugal and Sun Stalker, use the power of the heat shields to trap and kill the sharks."

Sun Stalker roared in approval. Klang Krugal called out to his monkeys, "If *Avrah* is with us, who can stand against us?"

That answer was soon found out. The cyclone struck. Winds carried at least ten monkeys from the trees. Waters claimed at least three leopards, who fought the currents that ate them. The poor beasts activated their heat shields too late, only to drown before the sharks even made it to shore.

Still, the savannah animals held steady. Yanta trumpeted her grand assault. The African elephants stampeded the waves. Krylakis and the giant squids grabbed at the legs of a few calves, but the sheer weight and number of elephants was too much. The heat shields activated. The saucer-like dim yellow eyes of Krylakis reflected her moment of epiphany: she had miscalculated. The heat was enough to singe her tentacles and trap her squid army in a searing fire. Yanta and the mother elephants trampled the heads of Krylakis and her squids, crushing the giant monsters beneath their massive feet. Yanta and the elephants trumpeted their victory.

The sharks pressed forward in greater numbers. Xrata led the charge, heading straight for Sun Stalker. Two cheetahs pounced on the great white shark. The shark's massive body writhed, flinging itself from side to side to free itself from its predators. Yet, it was not the power of the beast of the waters that freed it from the attacking cheetahs so much as an energy shield that defended the shark champion from the assault. Xrata tore at the torsos of the cheetahs, crushing both at once in his unforgiving jaws. The blood trickled upon the fangs of the great white shark king as his cold, purplish-blue eyes stared right through the king of the lions.

"Are these the lords of the jungles, the fierce predators that rule over the harshest lands on Earth?" Xrata asked Sun Stalker. "You are nothing. Especially when compared to the all-encompassing power of King Blu."

"We are the fangs of *Avrah*," Sun Stalker said. "Not even Death can stand against us."

Sun Stalker roared. His lions pounced from below. The apes, led by Klang Krugal, pounced from above. The gargantuan great white shark writhed its body and flung its massive head to and fro, freeing itself from the lions. Shark lieutenants clamped their mammoth jaws upon the feet of the leopards and lions until Sun Stalker stood alone. For a moment, the lords of two worlds, one the lord of the jungle, the other the lord of the depths of the unfathomable ocean, stared at each other with steely wonder. Just as quickly, Xrata's jaws opened, closing upon the torso of the lion king. Sun Stalker's heat shield sparked, repelling the giant shark admiral. The shock, bursting in lightning webs around the massive commander, compelled Xrata's jaws to let Sun Stalker go. Klang Krugal and his legions swung around. The apes dropped large nanobot-filled rocks upon the sharks and squids. The nanobots, programmed by Yanta's Stampeders, were predators. They burrowed into the skin of the sharks and squids until the legions of King Blu retreated towards the waters. Xrata's shield faltered as the nanobots attacked. Xrata looked at the fallen lion lord, whose blood joined with the waters. The mighty admiral opened his massive jaws once more, but the nanobots were precise predators. The shark lord's shield fell. Yanta trumpeted the news and a motley militia of elephants, lions, and apes descended. Klang Krugal and his apes fought off the surrounding lieutenants. The lions drew blood from Xrata for attacking their lord. Zulta and her elephants trampled Xrata and any sharks or squids not lively enough to get back to the ocean waves. Beaten, Xrata retreated with what life the great white shark had left, back to the abyss.

Klang Krugal and his apes were the first to take up the battle cry of victory. The elephants trumpeted. The lions and cheetahs roared. But the cries were short-lived. Xrata and his squids were but the first wave. Xrata nodded, arching his back, crying havoc in his own predatory shark language.

A giant wave of living, tentacled ocean, filled with octopi, sharks, and even whales, surged forward. Even legions of cloned *imperators* found their way into the waters. Xrata had cried for reinforcements. The oceans were so abundant in life that, within moments, King Blu complied. Yanta and Klang Krugal took a moment to see how many more sharks and whales they saw, but there was always another just behind, in a wave that knew no end.

"Retreat!" Klang Krugal called out.

Yanta trumpeted the same to her lieutenants. The lions and leopards dragged Sun Stalker's injured body back. Klang Krugal assisted, picking up the body of the bleeding lion lord while still calling back for his apes to run.

"Follow us," Yanta called out in *Osine*.

A stampede of jungle animals sought to outrun a tsunami of sharks, squids, and whales. The wave grew ever closer, nearly crashing, but holding firm. The animals followed Yanta's animals to ever higher elevations of jungle until they saw not rock nor tree nor vine but a portal, purplish and spherical, as in the days of The Serpent War. Yanta's elephant scientists had pulled through. Klang Krugal, cradling Sun Stalker in his massive gorilla arms, looked back for just a moment. All that his father, Yorba, had built, all that the ape lords fought for, was about to become little more than another arm of the ever-expanding ocean. Klang Krugal wailed as he followed Yanta and her Stampeders through the portal to whatever salvation or perdition lay ahead.

In a matter of moments, *Klang Uktor* fell to the sea.

CHAPTER 13

Nayseerus-Ral
The European Alps

Fire Hoof stood atop the loftiest peak of The Western Alps, his antlers lighting in golden fire as the ever-enlarging black flock approached. Fire Hoof turned to Blood Scar, the embattled old brown bear general, for insight. Around them stood surviving bears, Heygar and his wolverines, and Proud Feather, a great golden eagle, and her kin. The numbers included the refugees from *Yvot-Sing* who traversed the forbidding deserts to find a new home in the Alps.

"The Night Eye delight in fear and confusion," Blood Scar said. "They are only here to survey our numbers. I would not entreat with them."

"Perhaps," Fire Hoof said to Proud Feather, "you can surround them in the sky. Once they delivered their message, attack. Leave none alive."

In the pulsating seconds thereafter, The Night Eye flew forward with unearthly speed.

"Who leads the survivors of *Seerus-Ungalore* in our stead?" the raven flock of *Seerus-Ungalore* asked. "Fly forward. Hear the decree of your mighty lord, the all-powerful King Blu."

Fire Hoof nodded to Proud Feather, who flew. With a shrill shriek, Proud Feather gathered her forces, eagles, hawks, vultures, and even Eurasian eagle-owls. As ponderous as The Night Eye's numbers were, filled with ever-circulating crows, ravens, and kites, the sable cloud looked diminutive next to the aerial army of *Seerus-Ungalore*.

"We have but one question," The Night Eye said. "Will you surrender as *Gola Dwyn* did, or will you feel the full wrath of the whale god?"

"We are not water animals like the snakes of *Gola Dwyn*," Proud Feather said. "We will fight."

"You might join our ranks, the fleet of birds," The Night Eye said. "King Blu has allowed the birds the remaining peaks of land once his ocean covers the world. You might survive, even if your allies must die."

"We are as one," Proud Feather said. "We will kill every creature of the sea that claims our territory as its own. We may die, but we will make sure that King Blu sheds bloody tears for his lost children before we fall."

"Fools of a feather," The Night Eye said dismissively.

"Not all fools are of the same feather," Proud Feather said, looking over his right wing. "Look around you, blind seers."

The eagles and hawks closed in, in record numbers. Vultures circled still higher, unconcerned whether the meat that fed them came from dead or undead bones. Proud Feather unleashed a shriek that stabbed at the heart of the sky. Hundreds, thousands of fowl–owls, herons, starlings, finches–birds past naming and past number, joined in the fray. Soon, The Night Eye's circling swarm bled ravens and crows that twirled down to the ground, only for the buzzards to intercept and feast.

The waves beneath the sky swelled. Sky became sea, and sea became sky. Wave crests reached high enough to knock some eagles and hawks from the sky. In the raging waters, Qylar the Hunter appeared, commanding not just the octopi but the sharks after great Xrata's fall. Qylar sent a legion of bull sharks in to consume any fallen fowl before the eagles and hawks rose from the ocean. Qylar ordered Jylar to have his giant clams ready to feed. They opened their great pink-white shells, swallowing the eddying tides, and any animal caught in them. Yet, even from over the vast ocean depths, Fire Hoof sensed something. His golden antlers glowed in fresh fire, their flames bright enough to vanquish even the darkest ocean mists.

Moments later, Qylar's scheming became clear. Surviving terror lizards from The Serpent War struck, including the grand *sarcosuchus imperators* that signaled the presence of their master, King Croc. The dinosaurs and bull sharks ate through the defenses of *Nayseerus-Ral* until only the ice stood in the way.

"Hold tight," Fire Hoof said. "Let the terror lizards and sharks face us on the ice. We can battle them by the water."

Proud Feather shrieked, calling the eagles and hawks back to the peaks of *Nayseerus-Ral,* a place so elevated even the ocean mists froze. Blood Scar growled, herding his brown bears away from the ice. Fire Hoof led the reindeer. Heygar ordered the wolverines back. All animal lords kept their eyes on Qylar and King Croc.

Qylar and King Croc eyed the ocean swells. As much as the shark and whale lord captains pressed the waves further, they could not overtake the ice.

"The higher elevations are impenetrable, high commander," King Croc told Qylar. "We need the whale god to spin the ocean in such fury that it swallows even the greatest peak."

"King Blu battles King Dryga," Qylar said. "The whale god is not to be disturbed. He explicitly told us to conquer *Nayseerus-Ral* by any and all means necessary. The key word, master crocodile, is *necessary.* Why create a storm when you can have the storm come to you?'

Qylar The Hunter pointed one of his giant tentacles skyward. Out of a black fire came forth the dragon lord, Feng. His scales were a smoky gray, caught between a deathly pallor and a singed sable. The eyes, like those of The Night Eye, were ghostly white. With the undead emperor dragon were the rest of his Dragon Guard, an entire fleet of undead dragon warriors.

"They've resurrected the dragon lord," Blood Scar said to Fire Hoof. "Not even my finest brown bear fighters can stand against pure fire!"

"Sometimes, great bear general," Fire Hoof said, "it is more honorable to run."

"To where?" Proud Feather asked. "The dragons have mastery over land, sea, and sky."

"Follow the ibex," Fire Hoof said. "At the very top nook of the topmost peak, there is a portal, a gift from the Stampeders of *Klang Uktor.* Great eagle king, fly us there."

"But how?" Proud Feather inquired. "My birds have circled the skies endless times and have seen no such thing."

From atop the peaks, a great elephant cry reverberated, so loud the ice shook.

"Queen Yanta?" Blood Scar asked.

"To the portal—quickly!" Fire Hoof ordered.

Proud Feather shrieked his cry of retreat, flying at full might. The eagles, owls, herons, and finches became a great, winged line of gold, white, and black, pointing the way. The dragons circled, spreading deathly black fire to the lands below them. Yet, not even the dragon fire could kill an entire herd. Hundreds of wolverines, bears, fowl, and reindeer made it through the portal, calling back to the animals that followed.

Moments later, all was black fire and ash.

If *Klang Uktor* fell by sea, *Nayseerus-Ral* fell by fire.

Gungsung Dor

Bear Mountain, Rockies, USA

King Dryga saw the mighty Ice Giant fleeing, running faster than any bear had ever run, searching out the high rocks of *Gungsung Dor*. Behind him loomed a storm with the teeth of a predator. Lightning became its fangs, thunder its mighty fins. Its fur became the gray-black storm clouds that ate sea and sky; its eyes, the gigantic, spherical reflections that sat in the middle of a body that never seemed to end.

"King Blu," King Dryga said to the gathered animal lords. "I can sense him." King Dryga looked at his witch mother. "The time is now," he said. "Father longs to feast on whale flesh."

"It is not so easy," Freyda said. "The trees have shown me: no one animal god can stand against the whale god and win. He is too powerful. All you can do is buy your subjects time."

"I choose to never live in defeat," King Dryga said. "Both Azaz and I will stand together. The whale god will have blood coursing down his body. Gather the animals and flee. If we cannot kill a god, we can make a god bleed."

"There is yet hope, king of *Animus Nor*," Silent Wind said. "My kinsman, the great Pale Ghost, guided us to form a portal. Yet, a *rulku* has beat us to it. The woman witch invites us, even the bears, to join her in her hidden kingdom. There, the animals can join for one last assault."

"Who is this *rulku* witch?" King Dryga asked.

"Ruth the Lawless," Silent Wind said.

"The wife of Wade Brigand," King Dryga said, thinking back to the man of honor who once slaughtered animals without premeditation. King Dryga thought for a moment before saying, "We have little choice. Gather the animals. Dasu, Snow Prophet, and Pale Thunder, lead the way. Moon Herald, run like you have never run before. Igru, join him in leading the charge. Freyda, lead Ice Giant and all the bears. Azaz and I will buy the fleeing bears more time."

King Dryga walked a few steps before turning back and saying, "I leave the nation of *Animus Nor* in your paws and talons. No greater paws and talons are there on all the earth."

"King Dryga, this is folly," Dasu said. "You heard Freyda. This will only end in your death."

King Dryga laughed. The spirit of Azaz ascended, turning the laugh into a roar. "Faithless hunter," Azaz said. "Haven't you learned by now who is king of kings?"

For a moment, The Blood Paw circled around their transfigured king, who stood taller, surrounded by a coat of scourge-like white fire. The sight was indeed awesome, like Azaz of old. Azaz roared in greeting, ordering his bears to run. The massive All-Bear, part cave bear, part grizzly, part animal, part spirit, all god, stood on his hind legs, roaring courage into the hearts of animals everywhere. Just as quickly, the grizzly king ran, faster than even the monster bear Ice Giant ran.

"My lord," Ice Giant said as he ran towards the fire bear.

"Follow my mother," the spirit of Azaz said.

Ice Giant found courage, if just for a moment, saying, "You do not know the terror that you face. Let me stand by your side."

"The future of the polar bears lies in how fast you can run," the spirit of Azaz said. "Leave the whale god to me. I have seen his eyes before. Now, he will see mine."

Ice Giant bowed in homage to his fallen lord. He then turned back and roared, beckoning the polar bears on. The ice quaked. The land ruptured as mist and shadow broke through the ice. Storm clouds, dark as blood run cold, thundered the arrival of their king. Within a few flashes of pale lightning, the eyes of King Blu appeared. King Dryga watched as the monstrous primordial whale, part blue whale, part leviathan, breached the waters of *Animus Nor*. King Dryga felt the life fleeing him with each frozen breath. Yet, the power of Azaz held his eyes as the two gods eyed one another in timeless terror.

"Whale god," the spirit of Azaz said. "This time, I burn with a fire no sea can kill."

"The hubris of the Father Bear," King Blu said in a piercing whale song.

The song of the whale of death shook the ice further until King Dryga saw himself standing on a broken peak of a sea-eaten summit.

"You were the firstborn of *Avrah's* womb," King Blu continued. "Yet, what did you do with the sapient spark that gave you your awakening? Slaughter and more slaughter. In life, you were blasphemy. In death, you could have been my greatest weapon. Yet, unlike my faithful crows, you were rebellious to the core. Now, *Animus Nor* shall see your fire die as a sign. No one opposes the whale god and lives. Watch your son die and with him, the kingdom you squandered for blood."

"Enough talk," the spirit of Azaz said. "We'll see if you're so impudent when your flesh bleeds from my claws."

Azaz The Terrible stood up on his hind legs, sounding a battle cry that shook the waters nearly as much as King Blu shook the ice. In that thunderous moment, it was as if all the rage, anger, and wrath of the gods had poured itself from the heavenly mists into the spirit of the Father Bear. King Blu looked upon the white, electrifying aura of the bear god. Azaz, inexplicably, stretched his energy field until he doubled the size of King Dryga, the largest grizzly bear to ever live. On land, only an African elephant might outweigh the bear god. Yet, even then, the storm of lightning raging around the spirit of Azaz would have sent the beast running.

King Blu fought to submerge. Azaz growled, sending his lightning-like aura over the whale god. For the first time that King Blu could remember, an energy field nearly matched his own. The whale god knew that his sister, *Avrah*, must be working through the energy of the bear. Still, Azaz was only one piece of *Avrah*. King Blu wrenched himself free of the field. King Dryga growled, jumping from the ice into the sea. The difference in size between the largest of grizzlies and the lord of the whales was staggering. King Blu eclipsed the combined force of King Dryga and Azaz on every level. Yet, there was a raw power to the bear god that King Blu could not entirely shake himself free of.

The black and white orca stripes down the whale god's impossibly massive gray blue-gray back became a reflection of the greater light. The white-blue-gold light of the divine being shook until lightning sprouted and struck out in all directions. Even the massive, electric white light aura surrounding King Dryga felt the impact of the first whale of Creation. Dryga toppled back, the water greedily pulling him from the ice. King Dryga fought to hold the wet ice at every step. Yet, the power of the ocean was too great.

"Leave, now," the spirit of Azaz said to his son.

"I must fight," King Dryga said.

"This is a battle between gods, my son," the spirit of Azaz said. "Now go. Be the king I never had the chance to be."

Azaz, in his full, short-faced bear form, stood taller than the highest wave. Red, gold, and white flames cascaded in lightning fires down his back. What was once mass and fur was now a current of endlessly crackling fire, constantly consuming itself, only to spit out mightier flames. The burning fire of Azaz was a sight to behold, nearly as massive as Wylaka before the mighty orca king's fall. The bear god looked unnatural; even King Blu hesitated a moment at the sight.

"Well, whale god," the spirit of Azaz said. "Show me the meaning of death."

King Blu lunged from the waters. His body mass was a small sun of white, gold, and blue that approximated the form of a whale, only to consume itself in a new fire. With each turn of his massive body, the ocean quaked, sending in greater and greater waves. The bear god was there to meet the massive whale god at each turn of fire on the water. Even in his spirit form, Azaz mauled at the considerably more massive body of the great king of whales. Azaz's claws left fresh, burning scars on an already immense fire. King Blu retreated, if only for a moment. The great whale god sought to breach anew. Azaz mauled and butted the massive whale god. Yet, the awesome power of the animal god of death was too much. Soon, King Blu's greater fire consumed the roaring fire of Azaz. The bear god growled freshly as the flames swallowed him, and he disappeared.

"Father," King Dryga called back.

Yet, the cry was like a flame lost in the middle of a tidal wave. The cry, like the bear god, thundered and then vanished.

Remembering his father's words, King Dryga retreated from the ocean. Azaz's absence weakened the bear king in body and spirit. King Dryga looked back to see the eyes of the whale god staring after him. The otherworldly eyes looked as if spherical globes of earth had been set afire. King Dryga shuddered, certain that even a glimpse of the eyes would slay him. Yet, in that fire, Dryga saw, for the first time, weakness. Something of Azaz had shaken the unvanquished god, if only for a few fleeting moments.

King Dryga averted the eyes, running limply through the portal. As he did, King Dryga saw the entire body of King Blu hovering over mist and ocean. The blue-gold-white fire crashed below. In the shaking that followed, the seas consumed the heart of *Gunsung Dor*.

In the tides that ebbed were hundreds, thousands of animal bodies–unheralded and unsung.

CHAPTER 14

Gungsung Dor
Bear Mountain, Rockies, USA

Among the thousands of bodies left in the wake of the massive whale's god strike was one deserving to be sung above all others. Sky Death, the wisest of advisers, knew that death was near before Snow Prophet's owls said as much, looking over his shredded wings and punctured torso. For many, death was a fearsome shadow. For Sky Death, it was the rattling and the wetness that overtook his heaving body and made him ask to spend the last of his breaths paying homage to the rising moon. At first, the owls and eagles chattered amongst themselves, wondering if the once sagacious bird had finally lost his keen intellect. Yet, when it was apparent that the turkey vulture would never fly again, King Dryga honored the request. Sky Death knew that such a death was not a lonely one. He had fought long, lived fiercely, and cried boldly in unvanquished skies. Little more could a bird ask than to be *Avrah's* wings in the limitless heavens. And so, Sky Death waited, not unlike he did so many moon cycles ago, when he first saw the white wolf.

How thin the feathers of memory were, like blooming plumage on nestlings who have not yet taken their first flight. To Sky Death, it was as if those memories were breathing right next to him, clinging to the same air, fighting for the same life. And how the wise old bird remembered: he circled over the near frozen animal half-buried in the snow. Bathing in the sun of the South, Sky Death, an old turkey vulture with a wrinkled red head, a powerful, blood-stained beak, and claws of iron, had felt the same inkling he imagined drove this domestic, or *sss-hress,* as his kind called it, into the wild. After flying over two hundred miles off of carrion that littered the northern climes, Sky Death had been grazed by bullets to his right wing, which had a span of over three feet. The old vulture had a knack for survival, however, and lived to feed on the bodies of the *Hress,* as some vultures called humans, to avenge himself. His committee of vultures, in the new speak, or *Sezzus,* nominated him to leave the wake of the feeding young as he entered his twenty-fourth hunting season, as vultures now counted time, and thus could not live up to his fearsome name much longer.

In slow and steady circles, Sky Death descended upon the mass of fur, camouflaged as it was in the white of the snow. His nostrils flared and his beak readied, but the moving to and fro of the rib cage of the *sss-hress* kept him at a distance. Sky Death had a knack for finding the freshest kills, but until what some animals called *The Harkening,* he had never made a fresh kill. The men his kettle had surrounded had been the first, and two bullets later, Sky Death had fed enough to know that these *hress* were still more dangerous than any prey he'd ever seen.

A quick, jolting growl, and the *sss-hress* was up on its legs, its teeth bared as it readied itself to pounce.

Sky Death spread his wings to their full span and hissed, vomiting parts of men at the dog the way all turkey vultures did when threatened. Just as quickly as this defense tactic kicked in, the instinct left Sky Death and he and the poised *sss-hress* stood facing each other, circling, ready to pounce.

And now, after all these moons, here she was again.

"White wolf," Sky Death said, his eyes closing. "After all these moons, can it be?"

Glorious white fire, bundled in translucent fur, crackled all around him.

"Hello, my oldest and truest friend," Moon Shadow's spirit said. "So many suns ago, you found me in the arctic snow. Now, I find you to guide you to The Great Nesting Ground beyond. And I have not come alone."

Moon Shadow's eyes, gold on white, glanced upwards. There, in the night sky, Sky Death saw the dance of the moon. Great, sweeping clouds–surreal, mystifying, and beautiful–became as the wings of a mighty fire eagle as the moon took full form. The clouds extended, then retracted, as the moon waxed, then waned, until it was an impossibly perfect crescent that poked at the darkness and poured the starry light that spilled out from the sky over the waters below–over Sky Death himself.

"I always thought," Sky Death said, "that I would die alone, an old bird preyed upon by the fury of nature."

"Nature sings today," Thunder Killer called from above, "to honor the passing of the wisest turkey vulture that ever flew. Mighty Sky Death, you are known to the ancestors of all birds. You sit in a nest second to none. For *Avrah* and the spirit birds chose you for a venerable destiny, and that destiny is now fulfilled."

Two small barks, juvenile and full of the same fire as their mother, took to the sky.

"Sky Death," Moon Shadow said, "meet Laughing Cry and Shadow's Light, my two pups."

Sky Death looked upon the small bundles of white fire, unable to believe anything in Creation could have ever harmed creatures as precious as these.

"Lead on, white wolf," Sky Death said. "Fly on, noble eagle. Where you go, I shall follow until our three fires become as one."

Gola Dwyn, Animus Sur

The Amazon Rainforest

Thraxis sat staring over the occupying squid battalions when Mandau approached.

"What news, faithful captain?" Thraxis asked.

"King Blu has accepted the unconditional surrender of *Gola Dwyn*, Mother Empress," Mandau said with a slight trepidation in her hiss. "The city will be turned over to Admiral Xrata's forces by moonrise."

"I hear the frustration in your hiss," Thraxis said. "A snake never despairs, serpent commander. To survive is a battle; to live is a war. And one thing we snakes do very well is to survive. Another thing we do even better is to live at all costs."

"Yes, Mother Empress," Mandau said.

"Is there something more?" Thraxis asked.

"*Animus Nor, Seer-Ungulalore,* and *Klang Uktor* have all fallen," Mandau said. "The casualties are too vast to number, but we know this: among the dead was Azaz's adviser, Sky Death, the counsel of *Animus Nor*."

"Sky Death? That vulture lived so long I thought death had forgotten him," Thraxis asked. "How did the wise old bird meet his end?"

"Killing Commodore Wylaka with trickery," Mandau said.

"Then Sky Death died like a snake. He died well," Thraxis said.

"Yes, Mother Empress."

Thraxis studied the boa constrictor's eyes, still full of such fear and such disgust.

"There is something another wise old bird once taught me," Thraxis said. "Time is a river turned in upon itself, a snake eating its own tail. Sometimes, the only way to the future is to vanquish the past. Don't fear, Mandau. The snake's head will emerge again, and when it does, it will strike."

Mandau bowed her head to her fallen empress.

"Go now, Mandau," Thraxis decreed, "and tell the animal lords of the jungles to wait until the snake's head is ready to strike. I shall say when. The time for the mad queen to rise is almost at hand."

Mandau nodded her noble head and slithered off.

The moon rose all too quickly, announcing the birth of a new empire. Thraxis kept her watch well into the night, until she was sure that she was alone. After the dolphins and sharks waded deeper into the waters of The Golden City of Light, Thraxis saw her chance. So preoccupied were the agents of The Army of The Black Ocean that few thought anything of the whereabouts of a supposedly mad, fallen empress. It was as if the eyes of King Blu, awakened by his fight with Azaz, saw the bigger foe, the hidden *Avrah,* waiting to pounce. If ever there was a chance for Thraxis to test her convictions, this was it. She knew from her spies that King Blu had another crown—one not meant to rule, so much as to hone his energies when dealing with the landlings. The crown may not have had the same intent or power as the crown of the *rulku,* but it had some of the power of the whale god in it and that was power enough. And so, Thraxis took the red nanobot still in her possession and opened a portal to the open ocean, in search once again for the true Crown of Crowns.

Thraxis eyed the portal warily. For endless suns, Thraxis had postponed this moment. She had fought for a crown whose genetic mutations allowed a mad bear to spread bloodshed throughout the world. She had fallen prey to King Blu's trap, taking the trinket that supposedly made her the high queen of all animal life. But only upon losing the crown had Thraxis truly understood what Snow Prophet set out to teach her those many moons ago. A true empress is not the one who wears the crown. A true empress is the one who others follow even when there is no crown upon her head. And now, like Zehrah before her, the mad anaconda queen had to undertake the one journey that she was sure would end her life. Maybe not immediately. Maybe not in the great waters. But someday soon. The animal lords had each seen their hour, and precious few were left. But Thraxis chose to make her own end, not to let some mad whale god or misguided *rulku* hunter make the call for her. She chose to be the savior that the animal world needed, a snake not afraid to get a little blood on its tongue. And so, Thraxis gathered her courage and slithered through the portal. There was no other way.

Whereas before the seas were guarded by creatures more ancient than the light, now the deep-seated darkness was the primary sentry. Thraxis found that her white eyes, bound to the whale god, assisted her as she swam. Shark legions raced nearby; only the vast openness of the ocean saved her from a few near encounters. This would never have been the case in The Serpent War. It was clear that the whale god was not at his full might. Perhaps the bloody Azaz had served a higher purpose after all, after killing so many of her snake children. Thraxis could sense that the eyes of the great whale were not on her, but somewhere else, as King Blu nursed his own wounds and searched wildly for the evasive *Avrah*, mother of all things. Thraxis' serpentine lips stretched into something of a twisted smile. Finally, whatever snake spirits there were had blessed the great mother serpent.

And so Thraxis swam, the full pressure of the deep upon her armor. She marveled at the majesty of what in the common *Osine* tongue was known as *Emperia*, the crown jewel of the oceanic world. Even as the brilliant architect of *Gola Dwyn*, Thraxis marveled at the technological advancement of the under-water animals. In the years between wars, they had labored hard, dividing up the ocean barriers to limit access from the landlings above. But underneath, the cities were like massive coral reefs composed of perfectly clear energy that fueled each self-contained city—though, in truth, the cities were the size of nations. Each whale, shark, or dolphin pod had a clear, translucent tower of white that led straight to the surface where, unlike the primordial whale, they could slumber undisturbed. *Rulku* magic looked common—there were steel beasts everywhere, collecting algae, *rulku,* and unawakened fish dishes of all varieties for the masters of the deep. Underwater spheres, not unlike the one that arose to signal the end of The *Rulku* War, populated the city, providing warmth and energy and light to even the darkest waters. Brilliantly, the whales, dolphin, squid, and crabs had taken the sunlight and twilight zones of the habitable ocean and extended their influence downwards, allowing themselves to dwell at any part of the ocean they chose, from the deepest of trenches to the surface waters. Thraxis imagined that had it not been for the resourcefulness of the creatures of the sea, they might have invaded and overrun the coasts long ago. Even the great terror lizard abominations had their equivalents—towering mechanical beasts that looked like hybrids of Irukandji jellyfish, blue-ringed octopi, and Japanese spider crabs. A single brush against such guards as these would end even the great anaconda empress's life. In all of this, there were innumerable schools of fish of all colors, giant clams, crabs, sharks, and whales. It was almost as if every creature was part of the mind of the ocean, a part of King Blu himself.

Thraxis longed to steal what technological secrets she might, but even the mad empress had more sense than to give the scanning sentries any sense of her presence. She swam towards where the red nanobot summoned her, into the caverns below the edge of the city, towards an energy source derived from the original crown of the high kings. The anaconda had learned from her last attempt upon the realm of the whales. No prize could be so easily attained. Yet, to her surprise, Thraxis' brash brush with the apex predator of all life had left her with one distinct advantage since the last time she broached the ocean's depths. King Blu's attempt to transfer some of his energy into her, to drive her mad, to make her his sentry, had given her the appearance, to technology, anyway, of the whale god himself.

"Oh, how sweet vengeance is when it masquerades as justice," Thraxis thought.

An age before, King Blu had created false anacondas to set up the snake empress for her great fall. Now, here she was, masquerading as a whale whose energy and aura were part and parcel with the whale god himself. The caverns opened. The crown—not a *rulku* crown so much as a circular string of nanobots of dazzling blue befitting a whale—swam to her as if to its master. Thraxis looked around her, certain that the whale god's guards might pounce at any moment. Yet, in her cunning, Thraxis realized that she had chosen the single most opportune moment to attack. Perhaps the serpent spirits and the great spirit of Mother *Avrah* were with her after all. Before the giant abominations could sense her, Thraxis took her red nanobot and opened another portal. She swam from the light of the ocean to the darkness of the air of *Gola Dwyn,* emerging in the very spot she had left from. Closing the portals, Thraxis hid the red nanobot and slithered into the shadows. She must keep the crown of crowns upon her, undetectable, until the exact moment of fortune. And so, Thraxis tethered the crown to her mechanical arms, covering the blue energy with their own hard metal.

"I may die," Thraxis whispered to herself, "but if I die, whale god, a part of you dies with me."

CHAPTER 15

Klang Uktor
Congo, Africa

The wandering wizard sailed by raft, communing with the spirit of the water. Every atom, every particle of Creation, was sacred to the *rulku* that was not quite *rulku*, the outcast with the look of the whale god in his eyes. For many moons, Aeyra traveled, often under cover of night, searching wherever the heart of *Avrah* led him. And now, in the wake of a god ascended, Aeyra felt the need to kill calling him, to where he knew not. The wizard killer sailed deep into the watery heart of the jungle, undetected by the sharks and sea snakes that held the flooded *wenga* at bay. There, in the last watering hole not fully eaten by the sea, nestled in a shelter of fallen rock, lay the once proud leader of the elephant lords. He was still a giant, still white, still tattooed, still Zulta. Only Zulta was on the wrong end of boulders that crashed down where forest met savannah. The elephant king could not move. His body was broken, consigned to watching the sea creep ever closer.

"King Zulta The Half-Tusk," Aeyra said. "Can it be? Have I found you before Yanta's *Kami Kou* Stampeders?"

The tattooed white husk of a body looked limp, almost devoid of life. Zulta The Great lifted his head, then stretched his trunk as if to punch the air. The idea that a *rulku*, after all these wars, would be the one to kill him, was an irony the grace of an elephant could not withstand.

"Son of the death camp warmonger," Zulta said. "Has it come to this? Have you come to avenge a lost world order that will never rise again? If so, take my life, such as it is. But know that in the days of fire that raged not too long ago, I would have trampled you to death before you ever made it so close to me."

Aeyra pulled up in his raft and shook his head. He reached out his arm. The elephant lord sounded his trumpeting cry. Still, Aeyra approached, crouching near the fallen elephant lord.

"Your eyes," Zulta said. "They are not your father's. They are crazier."

"No," Aeyra said. "They are more ancient. They are my whale brother's."

Zulta struggled to lift his mighty head, to see the *rulku* wizard with fresh eyes.

"It can't be," Zulta said. "Could Zehrah, the horse that the great apes worship, have been right?"

"I am not her," Aeyra said. "I am a soul collector, a Charon, a boatman between worlds. I sail here, holy king, to bring you back to her from whose fire you were born."

"If you are here to kill me, call it what it is, *rulku*," Zulta said. "Either help it along or be on your way. I have seen more than my fair share of wizards for one lifetime, be they boas, bears, or *rulku* madmen."

"*Avrah* sent me," Aeyra said, "to be the terror of the world. I am to gather each flame to the greater fire, so that the fire of Creation may burn anew and consume the world."

"You are a wizard all right," Zulta said, "and you may be the craziest I've ever had the misfortune of meeting. Where is Yanta, my daughter? You haven't hunted her, have you, son of *Avrah*?"

"Yanta is a great leader," Aeyra said. "She should be. She has her father's blood. Yanta led your animals through the portal to safety before the whale god flooded your world. She lives as wisely as ever. That is why she is not here. *Avrah* sent me, but not to kill you. She sent me so that you would not die alone."

Zulta laughed, painfully. "Then the gods have a sense of humor after all," Zulta said. "If only I wasn't their punchline."

"You are loved by the ancient, endless elephant herd that calls you by name," Aeyra said. "You are loved by *Avrah*, and she needs you now."

Aeyra reached out again, touching the trunk and head of the massive African elephant, he of the mighty white body tattooed with the victories of his herd. The warmth of *Avrah* flowed through the long, bony fingers of the crazed *rulku* hunter. Zulta saw, for a second, lost like a flighty breeze to the incandescent wick of time, his herd standing before him. There were elephant spirits going all the way back to the first of suns. How tall they stood, how proud, how strong. Zulta smiled. The elephant lord knew that among the herd, his name was sacred. His battle–long, bloody, and unwavering–was, at long last, over. And so, Zulta looked one last time at the water-ravaged waste of the great open savannah where he was born. With one last burst of strength, Zulta trumpeted his farewell to the world.

Walking, half-shrouded by sunfire, was the shadow of the first awakened elephant lord. Zulta's soul stood tall amongst the most legendary of elephant lords, right where he belonged.

In the Andes, so many suns away, Yanta let out a cry–for what, she knew not. Yet, any animal alive that day can tell you that, even as the whale god conquered animal nation after animal nation, there was a cry so loud it shook the heart of the whale god himself.

Dyr Vespa
Andes Mountains, South America

A whole conclave of animal lords appeared on the ice-laden peaks of *Dyr Vespa,* stampeding around, trying to get their bearings. King Dryga, Ice Giant, Moon Herald, and Igru rounded up their young, while Fire Hoof, Blood Scar, Proud Feather, and Death Talon welcomed the latest arrivals. Also present, towards the uppermost peaks, were Yanta, Klang Krugal, and Sun Stalker. Flying overhead were Pale Thunder and Death Talon, and scurrying around them were Silent Wind, Pale Ghost, and Shadow Dancer, rushing to close the portal once the last four-legged beast ran through. King Dryga stood speechless when he saw the keeper of the portal, none other than the *rulku* queen, Ruth The Lawless, surrounded by *rulku* cubs.

"Can it be?" King Dryga asked. "Can so many *rulku* have survived our slaughter? Indeed, you are ferocious and cunning, like the mice magicians themselves."

"Gracious king of *Animus Nor*," Ruth The Lawless said, with a bow of her head. "We are all enemies of King Blu now, and that makes us brothers and sisters of the land. I brought you here as friends, not as enemies. The snakes have many old tunnels. And so does my assistant."

A mangy rat with long teeth and sickly yellow eyes stood forth.

"Preth the Pestilence, at your service," The Rat King said.

Yanta was tempted to scream. Yet, as eyes fell upon her, the wise African elephant said only, "We need as many animal friends as we can get. I am obliged to you, Preth, as are my herds."

"My *rulku* wizards saved you to set right what we did wrongly, generations ago," Ruth said. "Yet, even now, King Blu conquers the last of our lands. Even now, we must parley, great lords. We must decide where to stage our last great fight."

"Agreed," King Dryga said. "Yet, to kill the whale god takes greater power than any of us possess. Even Azaz fell before him."

"Have you forgotten your oracles?" Snow Prophet asked. "This is a fight for *Avrah* and her lords, not for mortal animals. Let Criddock, Freya, and I summon Methuselah and her witch sisters. Let us all decide the best way to face the whale god and win. If ever there is a time for the animal spirits to step forward, that time is now."

"What of the fallen empress?" Moon Herald asked. "It is said she has a direct line to the mind of the whale god. Why not ask her?"

"Our great black hawks tell us that Thraxis is still in the imperial city, *Gola Dwyn*, advising Xyla," Death Talon said. "King Blu's forces occupy the river city. It's too dangerous to reach out to her now."

"Whatever seers you have," Fire Hoof said, "let them meet without delay. The fire dragon Feng is reborn, with the eyes of death. Once King Blu discovers where the portals led–and he will discover the magic of the *rulku*–the whale god's full might will be upon us. The forces of *Gola Dwyn* and the strength of the sky dragons will be too much for us. We cannot afford to wait."

"The reindeer king is right," Klang Krugal said. He glanced over at Sun Stalker as the lion king fought for his life. "If ever *Avrah* is to stand with us, it is now."

Freyda The Fatal glanced over at Snow Prophet, whose eyes met Criddock's.

"Let us find a peak high up, undisturbed," Freyda said. "Whether it is from the tree witch or *Avrah* herself, we shall get an answer tonight."

"We leave our fate in your capable paws, Mother Bear," King Dryga said. "My Blood Paw guards will guide you."

"And I will guide them," Ruth The Lawless said. "These peaks are dangerous. Let Pale Thunder and Death Talon fly in watch. The rest of you can eat of the unawakened plants my men have gathered. Then, rest. My men and women are trained guards. Between them and the eyes of the hawks and eagles, we should have sufficient guard."

Freyda nodded. Snow Prophet flew just overhead. Criddock, for once, quickened his pace. Up the peaks they ascended, lost in mist and cloud.

CHAPTER 16

No Rul Ozu

Inyo County, California, USA

The great mother tree, singed and broken, glowed in a golden light. The magic of the golden nanobots circled like rogue stars among her as Methuselah conjured she knew not what. Her sisters, Jumon Sugi, Old Tijikko and Lady Diurnia among them, swayed in the lightning firing above them. King Clone, Pando, Lama, and The Mystic shook with such fury that their branches were like thunder on fallen sky. A magical wind, golden, translucent as gossamer at midnight, took to the air. The wind became an army, buffeting against the droplets of ocean. Not even the smallest saltwater particle infiltrated the ancient deserts of *No Rul Ozu*. Yet, the blackened branches of Methuselah served as a grim reminder: King Blu could not be held forever at bay.

"Does he know, Mother Witch?" Lady Diurnia asked.

"King Blu sees and does not see, all at once," Methuselah said. "It is impossible to see his godly mind. Yet, I suspect that the whale god has been in the body of the primordial male for so long that his mind thinks like a creature of the sea. He sees *Avrah* as only one body, with one face."

"Yet, even the greatest of secrets come to light," Old Tijikko said, swaying in the golden storm. "Perhaps it is time to confront the whale god once and for all."

"Not yet, my sisters," The Mystic said, reveling in the thunder. "When the animal lords make their stand in the land between lands, then we shall announce ourselves. We shall conjure a riotous thunder so loud even the whale god can hear it crashing into the sea."

"Through mists and winds and fires, through lightning and thunder and nightly eyes, the whale god shall swim, taken by surprise," Lama said.

"His own blindness will infuriate his pride," King Clone added.

"And then, we shall look him in his death-wielding eyes and see," Pando added.

"Either the whale god or we shall prevail," the seven sisters said. "The Holy Spirit calls to us, and we awaken. For always, we are *Avrah*; for always, we are life."

The golden storm surrounded the sundry forests and deserts. Its raining light hid even the mightiest of trees from detection in the naked light of day.

"And now, my sisters," Methuselah said. "I sense the cry of a bear, mountains away. I sense the call of the animal world."

"Answer the cry," Old Tijikko said. "It is time to lay down the seeds of their salvation."

The trees chanted. Through the golden storm, thousands of days' travel away, came the vision. Freyda and Snow Prophet and Criddock saw the great mother tree, inflamed in gold, pouring down its droplets of fire upon the stark desert sands, creating life. Nothing more needed to be said.

"The time is at hand," Methuselah said. "Journey towards Thraxis in the river city of Gola Dwyn. She holds the true crown, the one King Blu assumes must be in our possession. Let every animal lord make a stand. The empire of snakes waits to strike at the throat of King Blu's armies. They will see the shining crown as a beacon of light. King Blu shall see it as a beacon of his own doom."

"Against the vast numbers of The Army of The Black Ocean, none can stand," Freyda said, her witchy suspicions aroused. "Such a mission is suicide."

"To stand is to be victorious," Methuselah said. "You are but a distraction. My sisters and I are the true target. Once King Blu sees his mirror goddess, the final battle will be ours."

"Mother *Avrah*," Snow Prophet said in revelation.

Freyda, Criddock and the owl scribe all bowed.

"Have hope, my children," Methuselah said. "The spark of life ignites eternal. As long as a single tree grows, there is hope on Earth."

With that, the tree witches disappeared into the golden storm. The storm grew and grew, a mighty wind ready for a mighty wave. The storm winds expanded until they spread past the desert, heading to the sea itself.

Pali-Ko

Deep South Pacific Ocean

King Blu recuperated in the oldest den of the oceanic depths, letting the golden blue electricity of his aura heal the bear bites and scratches upon his gargantuan body. The massive underwater city of *Pali-Ko,* filled with intelligent coral, translucent shields that protected whales as they roamed, and entire populations of shrimp and other delicacies, swirled about him. Great octopi, sea horses, and great white shark soldiers all swarmed around the heart of the ocean, the mighty blue sun that was King Blu himself. And yet, as the whale god marveled at how far the oceans had advanced in just one generation, he thought back to when the waters were bare and all was new. King Blu thought back to the moment that blackness became light, the moment he became aware of his other half, *Avrah's,* presence in the primordial waters. He remembered that feeling keenly; he felt it again now.

Without *Avrah*, the bear king whose fiery carcass once fed Admiral Xrata and his legions would not dare to face him again. Yet, in the fire of this bear god of wrath, in the mauling that should have left no mark whatsoever, King Blu felt *Avrah's* touch piercing his flesh. The very touch alone scarred his body with marks no whale should bear. The thought occurred to King Blu that had never occurred as even a remote possibility before: he, the whale god, the apex predator of Creation, was vulnerable. In the ages before and since the tyranny of the *rulku, Avrah's* power had only grown. The fire must be extinguished before it lit a great many more fires that burned only too brightly. Yet, the issue of where and how to find *Avrah* and vanquish her grew more complicated. Part of the fire of *Avrah's* spirit was in the ancestral bear; another part of her fueled the very animal lords that King Blu meant to drown once and for all. But the heart of *Avrah*, that which gave life to the others, eluded the whale god. King Blu knew that his second half had cleverly divided herself among the very abominations she wished to save. Yet, snuffing Azaz was like cutting only one protrusion from a hundred-headed hydra. No, the whole creature must die in primordial fire. King Blu healed, entering a trance. He concentrated, sweeping the ocean, sky, and earth, searching out just where the heart of the earth might be. Yet, King Blu felt pulled in different directions, all across the earth. The presence of *Avrah* was there, but the power was not. It was a conundrum the whale god bent his entire mind towards, even as he rested vertically, sleeping as much as a god ever does. Until, in a mist of gold released to the air, the answer came to him, in a single word: Methuselah.

"Your holiness," the voice of the great pink octopus said, bowing.

"Yes, King Qylar," King Blu said, between strokes of whale song that shook *Pali-Ko.*

"My octopi interrogators have spoken to many reptiles from *Gola Dwyn,* including Empress Xyla herself, about the missing crown," Qylar The Hunter said. "I am convinced the treachery of the serpents of *Gola Dwyn* knows no bounds. They mean to strike–and soon. The empress herself is behind it, and I don't mean Xyla."

"Thraxis The Conqueror is but one face of *Gola Dwyn's* destruction," King Blu said, his song shaking the waters. "Let her live, for now. I have been experimenting in the deep waters, Interrogator. I have found an antidote to the pestilence *Avrah* sent to the ocean animals. I have spread it far and wide among the ocean waters. Everywhere but *Gola Dwyn.* Let the serpents think their tunnels and riverways give them the advantage for when the inevitable uprising occurs. I mean to draw the animal lords together for one last stand. There, while my champion fights the animal lords, I shall cripple the power of *Avrah,* using her own toxins against her. She shall sicken and die as she watches her animal lords fall for their hubris. This pestilence, a combination of the last deadly plagues, shall be more powerful than any other. And it shall target the complex plants of the earth."

"The forests, my lord?" Qylar the Hunter asked. "Would it not be more prudent to target the animal kingdoms directly, once and for all, before any further uprisings occur?"

"Tell me," King Blu said, "have you seen the sign of *Avrah* among their number?"

"Only in their legends," Qylar said. "Only in Zehrah."

"A puppet in the hands of a hidden puppeteer," King Blu said. "One the landlings themselves killed."

"They are foolish, your eminence," Qylar said. "No animal lords are powerful enough to stand against you and live. Even should they stand united, the battle would be a hopeless one."

"The animal lords are a front. *Avrah* hides herself among the plants," King Blu said. "*Avrah* is the earth and all that nourishes. It is the only explanation I can gather. We must broaden our target until *Avrah* begs for mercy. We must be ready for the final fight."

"Yes, great whale god," Qylar said. "Your wisdom is endless."

"Only death is endless, Master Interrogator, a lesson I mean to teach to *Avrah* herself," King Blu said. "In the meantime, hold a meeting for the snake lords. Say that you mean to give each a continent to oversee. Send them through the portals, dividing them. As you do so, the largest navy the animal world has ever seen will be on its way to *Gola Dwyn* before the first of their fangs strike."

"A navy led by whom, my lord?" Qylar asked. "News of Xrata's infestation has traveled the wide world, both above and below the ocean waters. He is presumed dead. The animal lords have grown confident that there is still hope when the champion of King Blu falls."

"A hope that I will soon annihilate," Admiral Xrata said.

The great white shark, scarred with the slices of nanobot plague, appeared in an aura of unearthly gray, white and blue fire. Xrata swam from the den of King Blu himself, healed and hungry. Thousands upon thousands of sharks massed behind him.

"Now go, Master Interrogator," King Blu said. "The time for *Avrah's* emergence is at hand. All must be in place for the ultimate battle of the gods."

Qylar the Hunter bowed before King Blu and his massing navy. Fearsome as he was, even the great octopus king, Qylar, trembled at the terror of King Blu's navy: one larger, with more ancient whales and sharks than any even Qylar had seen. As The Army of The Black Ocean formed behind the great shark king, Qylar summoned his octopi interrogators and swam off.

CHAPTER 17

Vygryn-Durn

The Edge of the Amazon Rainforests

Aeyra knelt in prayer, seeking to connect with the spirit of all that was. He felt the ferocity of the wolverine, the strength of the eagle, the cunning of the wolf, and the wisdom of the elephant guiding him, but the eyes that were on him were not those of the spirit world alone.

Soon, the air whispered.

The voice was not unfamiliar, like that of the ancient wizard Aeyra heard tell of. So long ago, when his father spoke to the man cub about the mighty steel beasts and the end of the reign of the *rulku*.

They will need your aura to hold the seas at bay, the air said in elaboration, *before the final blow.*

Aeyra knew not to ask. The vision came to him more clearly than the mists along the edge of the slit-like palms of the palla trees. There she was, Thraxis, about to take back the crown she had so resoundingly lost, the madness of the whale god fully upon her eyes. Aeyra felt in the pain of thought the connection to the mind that was so much greater, so much more ancient than his own. This, the whale god intended. Through Thraxis, animal civilization would live or die. Aeyra knew the vision came from *Avrah*. It was a warning, especially dire: Aeyra was the happy accident. He was the boy who saw the eyes of the whale god and lived. But he was a boy born of *Avrah*, and the mark of two gods was upon him. Aeyra understood the full gravitas of the warning. The animal lords would kill the young man before they would allow a *rulku* near the crown of Azaz and Thraxis. Yet, Aeyra was the only one who might wear the crown and magnify its power. Only then could the mighty flame of *Gola Dwyn* and *Animus* survive. Only then would some small spark of civilization swallow enough kindling to ignite the new animal world.

Aeyra concentrated, praying for further guidance on his sacred path. Yet, the eyes were always there, watching him from between the trees.

"If you plan to strike, strike and be done with it," Aeyra commanded in the old *Osine*.

The mountain lion King Dasu crept through the ferns, towards the slayer of the animal lords.

"You are wanted by the king of *Animus Nor* for questioning in the deaths of quite a few animal lords," Dasu said. "Stay where you are, or I will kill you where you kneel."

Aeyra, still kneeling, turned his head back to the darkness.

"You are right to fear me, king of the great cats," Aeyra said. "I am a man of terrible destiny, an instrument of justice in an unjust world. I'd say it's better that I die before another animal lord does. Yet, the spirit world seems to disagree."

"You are the killer of Groth the Impaler," Dasu said. "The nanobots circling Thunder Killer and Sky Death showed you around them moments before they flew to their deaths. Queen Yanta also claims that you were responsible for her honorable father's death. Just how many animals have you killed, *rulku*?"

"There it is," Aeyra said. "The fire of the fierce animal warrior, the one who hunted *rulku* with Azaz, who would have hunted them into extinction. I can smell the death upon your teeth, waiting to sink itself down upon my flesh. Strike then, exalted right paw of King Dryga. You will find out where the spirits of the animal lords dwell soon enough."

Dasu lunged. Aeyra sprung to his feet. Even with his back turned, Aeyra maneuvered out of the way. He moved like a ghost, as if *Avrah* herself directed his steps. Dasu circled the man beast, waiting to make his next attack.

"Tell me why, young beast," Dasu said. "You never saw the bloodiness and greed of the *rulku*. Whatever King Dryga decreed upon your father, it was a mercy by comparison. Your kind would have poisoned and killed the entire earth. So why do you kill, *rulku*? It's as the name suggests: it's in your blood, isn't it?"

The wind fluttered through the palla tree palms, as if in answer.

"There it is," Aeyra said. "The voice of *Avrah*. Some things must be simply because they must be. The wind that came just now came whether I lived or died. The golden storm winds," Aeyra said, pointing to the distant sky. "They come whether or not the great lord Dasu stalks his prey. That is my terrible destiny, Dasu. It comes because it must. In every vision, every morning, I see what I must do. And in every vision, *Avrah* shows me those who would prevent it from happening. There was Groth, who would impale me before letting me touch the crown. There was Thunder Killer, who would have plucked the crown with his talons before I could place it upon my head. There was Sky Death, who would rally the animal lords against any animal wearing the crown. And, of course, before all of them, there was Moon Shadow, the wolf queen of *Animus Nor,* who would've opposed me."

"*You* killed the great wolf queen," Dasu said. "I've seen her in battle. She was more than a match for any *rulku.*"

"She was tired and worn, a great mother of all to the end," Aeyra said. "*Avrah* took her. I only sensed it in my young skin."

"You lie."

"The spirit world will show you the truth."

"So now *Avrah* has shown you me prowling, mad *rulku,* is that it?" Dasu asked, still circling. "If so, *Avrah* has shown you your own death."

"My time is near at hand," Aeyra said. "My vision just now was not of you. That vision, of the mountain lion maddened with rage, haunted me the moment I entered the jungle. It stopped haunting me the moment you approached. My new vision is of the next animal lord who stands in my way. If this animal lord seizes the crown for herself, we shall all see–"

As Aeyra spoke, Dasu struck. The master of the mountain lions lunged at the mad *rulku,* if only in defiance of any *rulku* who would dare to wear the crown. Aeyra let the mighty weight of Dasu's striking body do the killing work for him. Dasu dove heavily into The Spear Of Black Fire, Thraxis' old weapon of choice. The blow was mortal, but Aeyra used the spear and stabbed at Dasu several more times to make sure Destiny had a clear path.

"–Ruin," Aeyra said in completion. "And so it is. Ruin surrounds us. You were a formidable foe, mountain lion lord. *Avrah* honors your sacrifice."

Aeyra bent down as Dasu, unable to gather the strength to even bite, took a few last breaths. Aeyra saw a vision of the hunting of the *rulku,* of the liberating of the pets, of The *Rulku* War, of The Serpent War. Dasu had been so strong for so long.

"Rest," Aeyra said, in *Osine.* "Look out upon the beauty of the jungle. See the natural beauty of death."

Dasu calmed, if but for a moment, as if back in that time before time, before The *Rapsys.* Dasu saw the wonder of life, even in the enigma of death. Quietly, the wind drew forth, fluttering past the palla tree palms. Whether that wind carried with it the spirit of the mighty mountain lion lord, who could say?

Tyr-Valon

Amazon Rainforest

Yanta trumpeted for her Stampeders to watch for any snakes underfoot. Unfortunately for Yanta, the snakes were already watching her. The crafty boa Mandau, spy of Xyla and servant of Thraxis, had silently slithered through the tree branches and had her army at the ready.

"Silence is the secret of survival," Mandau said. "You animal lords are anything but. What is your plan, exactly? To march into the greatest living city on the planet and challenge its unvanquished ruler, the god of death, to a battle? How exactly do you think that will go?"

"Snakes," King Dryga said. "So ready to trade honor for survival."

"And now the lord of the lost *Animus Nor* seeks to alienate his only allies?" Mandau asked. "If you were snakes, this war would be going better. A snake knows when to strike and when to slither."

"Allies? You surrendered to the whale god without a fight," King Dryga argued. "And for what? Snakes drown just as bears do."

"Not all is as it seems, bear king," Mandau said. "A snake is a master of knowing the subtle difference. You must be too. Our enemies are nearly where they need to be for us to strike. Thraxis has sent me. She asks you to hold up in the rainforest until the time is at hand. The whale god grows suspicious. His great inquisitor, Qylar The Hunter, has questioned many serpents. Orders now come for our serpent lords to be relocated. The uprising is imminent. We will need you soon."

"And if we strike now," Klang Krugal asked, "with the element of surprise?"

"All will be lost," Mandau said. "I know you don't trust snakes, but if ever there was a time to trust, that time is now."

The animal lords, strange creatures in an even stranger jungle, looked at one another and at their palm-laced surroundings. King Dryga noted multiple boas along the trees, anacondas at the perimeter, and vipers at their feet. Not one paw-length lacked a pair of eyes, watching. The expression in the eyes of Yanta was the same as in the eyes of Klang Krugal, King Dryga, and Sun Shadow. It was too dangerous to fight a war with an invisible enemy.

"What choice do we have?" King Dryga asked. "It would seem you have us surrounded. If we fight now, we stand no chance of winning later."

"Empress Thraxis thought you would say as much," Mandau said. "I have been authorized to give you a brief transmission to reassure you of our good will."

Mandau nodded towards a boa spy. The spy activated a crude approximation of what was once the nanosphere, before the water ate the lands.

"Honorable lords," Queen Thraxis said.

The giant pale green anaconda, still clinging to life, looked taut and wrinkled, but still burned with a bristling white aura of the indomitable. A fallen empress she may have been, but a fallen empress was still an empress–and this empress stood at least ten feet tall.

"I assure you that you play into the plans of the whale god," Thraxis said. "You have heard rumors of my madness, of my displacement, of a smashed crown. I assure you that rumors of my madness have been greatly–well, slightly–exaggerated. King Blu must think he has shaken my mind from its very foundations. He must think that Xyla reigns and that the forces of Qylar and the octopi occupiers have numbered our legions correctly. This is the army he prepares to vanquish. My sea snakes assure me that the scuttlebutt of the sea is that King Blu counts on you to take a stand against him. When you appear, he will strike with his full might to kill the children of *Avrah* and wipe them from the Earth. You must stand as planned. From tunnels below the ocean, my true navy will strike: terror lizards of such proportions as the world has never seen. They will keep the admirals of King Blu occupied and give you a fighting chance against Feng and his dragons—until my magic claims them, that is. As for the whale god himself, our connection is not one-way only, as the whale god seems to believe. I see his intent. King Blu means to draw out *Avrah* to confront her once and for all. Only *Avrah* can stand against King Blu and hope to prevail. All we can do is give her time to work her magic. The spirit animals will do the rest. Thus, we arrive at this critical hour. I beg you: stand down until my commander, Mandau, tells you to march. Then press on with all of your might."

The hologram of the great snake empress faded. Mandau and her boas looked directly into the eyes of the king of *Animus Nor.*

"I can't believe this is possible for a bear to say," King Dryga articulated after a solemn moment of silence. "Yet, we will trust you. Your plan greatly exceeds ours."

King Dryga, Ice Giant, and Freyda roared at the bears and other land animals to halt.

As the king did so, a flurry of black crows, kites, and ravens flew overhead.

"The Night Eye," Snow Prophet said. "The eyes of King Blu."

"They fly to report our location and our plan," Klang Krugal said. "We must send our eagles to kill them."

"Undoubtedly, they fly to betray us," Criddock said. "Yet, I would not be so hasty to kill. You assume they saw the transmission. I would not be so sure. Sometimes, an impassioned lie can be more persuasive than the truth."

"How can you be so sure they didn't hear and see everything?" Sun Stalker asked. "The Night Eye, of more flocks than there are stars, sees all."

"Witches of a feather," Criddock said. "While you spoke, Freyda, Snow Prophet, and I wove our magic. We created a vision so vast, so powerful, it would send The Night Eye scurrying."

"What could have such power?" Queen Yanta asked.

"We worked with Ruth's magicians to multiply our numbers by holographic illusion," Snow Prophet said. "King Blu will expect an army of hundreds of thousands of animals, much bigger than he anticipated. The odds The Night Eye figured out which hologram was the true Thraxis are quite slim."

"Won't such a false report just hasten our doom?" Fire Hoof asked.

"King Blu will send his mightiest to the fore too early," Freyda The Fatal explained. "Thraxis' army will be ready to lay waste to the best the whale god has to offer."

"So we hope," Snow Prophet said. "The whale god is as cunning as he is ruthless."

"I'll take a little hope over no hope at all," King Dryga said. "So far, a little hope is more than we've had to feast on in ages."

"Very true," Moon Herald said. "If we are to stay, we might as well set up camp and feast. Who knows when the snakes will sound their call?"

The animal lords nodded in assent. Then came the hardest part of war: the endless waiting.

CHAPTER 18

Gola Dwyn
Amazon River Basin

Thraxis coiled herself in her den, sleeping, when she sensed the *rulku* in the air around her.

"*Rulku* are so inelegant," Thraxis said, opening one eye. "They stumble when they should slither and reek, filling the air, when they should be as unassuming as a river breeze. Yet, my child, I am happy that I taught you well. You have made it past even the cunning snake sentinels unscathed. I imagine that you deprived them of their senses. You are a true killer now. Everything I brought you up to be. A mother couldn't be any prouder than I am of you right now."

"Proud," Aeyra said, holding out his unwashed hands. "I wonder if you knew all along that I was the boy killer. I wonder if you knew how much blood Destiny would put in my path."

Thraxis raised half of her body up. She opened her eyes. Old as it was, Thraxis's green-black body still smarted in the white aura of a god. Aeyra could feel the snake's eyes upon him. They were as cold as ever, as full of death as his own eyes.

"You needed to have a stomach for what lay ahead," Thraxis told him. "The whale god will show no mercy. Your blood, to him, is but a pollutant in the sea."

"You must know why I am here," Aeyra said. "You must feel it in your skin."

"So, you're how it all ends," Thraxis said, almost as if relieved. "After so long a life, after seeing the mightiest of rivers and the largest of deserts, after traversing the sea and looking into the eyes of the god of death himself, Destiny has brought you to me." Thraxis hissed a quick laugh. "Or is it me who has brought you to your destiny?"

Aeyra gazed at the snake empress in unholy wonder. At the moment when Thraxis' eyes met his, they saw the moment those eyes shared with the whale god so many sun seasons ago. At that time, Aeyra was simply a young *rulku*, barely able to swim up towards King Blu to intervene for his snake mother. Now, the years had settled as thickly on him as the matted jungle. Despite the *rulku's* sinewy strength, Thraxis questioned whether he was truly ready for the task that called to him like she had so many moons ago.

"You realize that you are the key to this," Thraxis said. "You and I have seen the eyes of the whale god, however briefly. The crown will recognize only us as its ruler. And to wear the crown is to join your thoughts, however momentarily, with those of the whale god. He will seek to dominate one of us, to drive the chosen crown bearer to madness. If King Blu wins, he will flood the entirety of *Gola Dwyn* and kill the animal lords in a single blow."

"I know all this," Aeyra said. "I also have had another vision, one where you will stand in my way. You use me to bring the true crown one more time, Mother, in its full potency. Your moment of weakness causes the animal lords to fall. That is why I am here. I have come to thank you for all you did for me. And I have come to take your life so that everything you fought for since The Serpent War might come to pass."

"You certainly have visions from *Avrah*," Thraxis said. "The question is, are you interpreting them correctly? Why not let *Avrah* decide? Strike me with your full might. See whether I live or die."

Aeyra bowed before the great serpent, who now fully extended herself. The *rulku* warrior lifted The Spear Of Black Fire. Just as quickly, he lowered the jagged blade upon the head of the snake. The blade went right through Thraxis's neck—or, at least, that of her hologram. Aeyra stumbled back, searching, when half a dozen apparitions of the great anaconda surrounded him. The dazed *rulku* closed his eyes, concentrating, seeking to sense the presence of the real empress. Aeyra waited too long. The real Thraxis struck from behind, strangling every ounce of the young warrior's body.

"You are special," Thraxis said. "I won't kill you, my son. I will let you wait in the waters like a beacon in the sea. The Night Eye must see you, must descend ever so close. We will rid ourselves of the last of that malicious flock that serves as the eyes of the whale god. The hour will come for my children to be set free. Then you can live or die, as I see fit."

Thraxis nodded to two anaconda servants, who slithered through the jungle. They hoisted the *rulku* body upon their fearsome backs and slithered after their empress into the dark of the fallen vines.

Syk Entor
The Southern Ocean

The greatest cloud of sky, sea, and storm the world had ever known thundered ahead of the Armada of the Ocean as if a fife of fortune. Untold legions of flying fish and aerial manta rays, sparkling in the blue, gold, and black of the whale god, swarmed the air. Behind them, King Croc's half-*rulku,* half-crocodile monstrosities rode mighty *mosasaurs,* rising and falling with the tides. At their side swam the giant octopi, some thirty feet long, flanked by even more humongous giant squids. At the rear of the mighty fleet were the great white sharks, with Admiral Xrata swimming anonymously among their number. Lastly, the whale ambassadors themselves, from orcas to northern right whales to the mighty blue whales, formed an impenetrable perimeter. Above them, in the sea of sky, flew Feng and The Dragon Guard. Above them all, with a watchful gaze, fluttered The Night Eye, heralds of the end times.

"We are approaching *Gola Dwyn* within a sun's migration," Admiral Xrata said. "What are your orders, god of all animals?"

"The manta and flying fish shall be the first to swarm the animal lords," King Blu said. "King Croc's legions follow next."

The waters shook and boiled with the power of the whale god's song.

"I shall create a new ocean in the jungles of *Gola Dwyn,*" King Blu said. "Have your sharks and whales ready to finish off whatever does not drown."

"As you wish, my lord," Admiral Xrata said.

"The animal lords will aim for more trickery," King Blu said. "I will swim close enough to disarm their portals. Be ready. I shall rely upon you. I must swim to the western waters. I know where *Avrah* lies. Her golden storm announces that the time for the last battle is at hand."

"The goddess challenges?" Xrata asked. "In the flesh?"

"*Avrah* divides her power among her children," King Blu said. "It is no matter. She shall fall. *Avrah* shall join with her creations in spirit and the world shall be made new as when the first oceans sprung from the air."

"Yes, my lord, "Admiral Xrata said. "Only–how do we who are not gods survive the golden storm, master of the sea? Thus far, not even the most durable terror lizards have been able to stand against it. The winds rain fire down upon the bodies of your children. None can survive."

"I will survive," King Blu said.

The certainty of the song shook the deep black waters.

"I will challenge the storm and bring it with me back to its origins, back to Methuselah, the hidden *Avrah*," King Blu said. "Her own fires shall be her destruction. You needn't worry. Now go. Show the landlings the power of the sea."

With that, Admiral Xrata turned to the terror lizards. The *mosasaurs* roared, and the armada swam until the spiraling towers of the river city were within sight, until the first of Thraxis' flying machines formed a perimeter. *Gola Dwyn* was ready for a fight, the admiral saw. Yet, even the animal lords knew: not even the jewel of the animal world could withstand the pulverizing hammer that was King Blu's Army of the Black Ocean.

CHAPTER 19

Sulka-Ra

Amazon River Basin

On a cliff above a lonely coastline, well ahead of the marauding armies of the sea, stood Aeyra. The boy who somehow withstood the whale god, now a man beast in full form, threw The Spear Of Black Fire. The spear opened, releasing thousands of tiny serrated nanobots with golden fire snares strong enough to still the undead wings of the ravens. Aeyra simply watched as the nanobot snares swarmed upon the last ravens of The Night Eye. He let the snares surround the birds, pulling away key members, so that The Night Eye stumbled for words. At first, The Night Eye, consumed with their greater task, paid the *rulku* wizard no heed. Then, more of their flock fell to the mysterious snares. As more of their message fell apart, The Night Eye descended upon Aeyra for a frontal assault.

"Disgraced man beast," Mother Raven said from above. "What threat can you be to us, who are as numerous as the stars of the sky, painted black? You will fall, like all of your kind, as The Epoch of the Whale begins."

Aeyra chanted. The Spear of Black Fire wrapped back around, singing through the air as it split more and more crows, ravens, and kites in two.

"I was born of a killer," Aeyra said. "The blood of a killer flows through my veins. What's your excuse?"

Elkira, the mother raven, saw the eyes of the *rulku* and realized who it was.

"You are among the first *rulku*, the most evil of *Avrah's* wayward children," Elkira said.

"That is all the excuse we need. Descend, ravens," Elkira chanted, as her sister ravens joined her. "Peck out the eyes of the unnatural beast. Swarm him! Make my words a prophecy: his blood shall paint the ocean waters."

The ravens descended, a blackening waterspout of talon and claw. Yet, Aeyra didn't move. The strange *rulku* set his eyes on the white-clouded eyes of The Night Eye. The eyes of The Night Eye fought him, but some residual magic of the whale god, some divine touch, lost between Aeyra's dead eyes and the ra-vens' dead eyes, sparked life. As if held in a witch's spell, The Night Eye lit up in black fire. The fire raged into a burning cloud that reached armlike around the flock and around Aeyra, holding them in the same magical space.

"It's a battle of witches, is it?" Elkira asked.

"This magic is beyond me and beyond you," Aeyra said.

"Nothing is beyond The Night Eye," Elkira said, lunging with the last of her flock.

Yet, not even the power of the great bird sorceress herself could break the ancient magic that bound them. Instead, in the black mist between *rulku* and raven, a giant shrouded body emerged and with it, the ghostly echo of two fiery eyes in the shape of spheres. The spheres bulged out in their fire, threatening to consume Aeyra and The Night Eye whole. Even so, through skin-smoldering pain, Aeyra held his gaze. The thoughts of the whale god, momentarily, poured into the mists. Aeyra saw the giant squids and terror lizards ripping *Gola Dwyn* from its foundations, tossing bloody bear limbs to the sea. The whale god him-self swam at full speed, awesome and alone. The mind of King Blu was fixed on one location: the deserts of *Animus Nor.* King Blu flooded the lands in front of him until he stood face to face with Methuselah. Aeyra fought, but the will of the whale god was too great. Seeing through the eyes of his harbinger birds, King Blu broke through the mists until only ashes and embers remained.

The Night Eye broke free. Their eyes came to life again, with renewed flame. Yet, Mother Raven cried, and the entire flock descended upon Aeyra. Aeyra summoned The Spear of Black Fire, but even a slicing blade was too late. The assault of the birds was too much. Aeyra covered his eyes, letting his arms, hands, torso, and legs shield what was left of him from the mad assault of the ravens, crows, and kites. The Spear of Black Fire sliced through Elkira. The loss of their mother left The Night Eye vulnerable, raven crashing into kite and kite into crow. Aeyra, in a last effort, threw his body from the cliffs into the open ocean. He kept below the surface, using his gills to full effect. Aeyra let his blood paint the waters red, exactly as The Night Eye had prophesied. The Night Eye focused their energies on gathering their undead mother's body. The ravens uttered spell upon spell of binding magic. Elkira remained lifeless. The Night Eye, remembering the greater charge, regrouped. They carried Elkira's body with them as they flew off. King Blu's message burned their feathers worse than the fire mists that so nearly tore them. The message, so searing, must be delivered: *Turn over all snake lords or pay the ultimate price.*

No Rul Ozu
Inyo County, California, USA

There was a burning in the air that smelt like the fires of first creation. Methuselah could not pinpoint it precisely: too many ages had passed, forming the arid sands where plants fought the natural world for survival. Too many moons had risen and fallen like hallowed sacrifices to forgetful gods. Yet, there was something in the air–ancient, primordial–that Methuselah had not sensed since the time when she and her lost twin god were two fires raging in the same smoky womb.

"King Blu has found us," Methuselah announced to her sisters.

The sisters swayed in symbiosis, some on rocks of fallen continents, surviving through the sheer will of *Avrah*.

"He rages from the heart of the sea," Old Tijiiko added, "a fire that no god can tame."

"Long have we felt his heart," Pando said, "like a hammer striking against its own forge."

"His heart is strong," Jumon Sugi added, "but ours is stronger still. If he is the sea, we must be the fire water beneath the sea–the deep, flame-lit ocean of lava that destroys to create anew."

"Yet, what is his power without ours?" King Clone asked.

"And what is ours without his?" Lady Diurnia responded.

"We shall soon find out," The Mystic prophesied. "For it is said, sisters, that one's death is the other's life, and that one's life is the other's death. We are two faces of the same fire eating its own flames."

"The Golden Mist returns," Lama called. "King Blu is almost upon you, Methuselah."

The mystical trees grew pensive and quiet. They sensed, in mists they had not felt in eons, the closeness of the sea. With each revolution, the great whale god raised the waters over lands that had been dry for so long that even the cacti had to think back upon when they last suckled upon wayward rains. Yet, Methuselah waited with the patience of a mother. She remembered back, across lives, when she was a speck floating in a hostile land, a microbe seeding the sea. Methuselah remembered back to when her children took to the land. She remembered creating with the earth the lush vegetation that had once surrounded an ancient world. Yet, here Methuselah was, feeling like a seedling after so many thousands of arid years. King Blu drew ever closer. The storms signaled his arrival. Not even the prophetic tree witches could say what might happen when the two gods met. Perhaps one world would die; perhaps another would be reborn. Methuselah held firm. The waters inched closer, covering the future like a nascent jellyfish beneath deadly, misshapen tides.

CHAPTER 20

Gola Dwyn
Amazon River Basin

Gray-black storm clouds, bursting with golden red fire, crackled as far as any animal eye could see. The ocean, riled and treacherous, heaved to and fro in the thunderclouds. The empress Xyla, with Thraxis at her side, appeared as commanded upon the shores of the great snake river. Among the black, tiny, speckled points of light emerged the undead eyes of The Night Eye. The harbingers of King Blu flew forward in a fluttering mass. Just above them, flying in full circles around the cloud, were The Dragon Guard and its emperor, the undead Feng. Thraxis looked up in supplication at her children, so high in the skies that they looked like jagged multicolored bolts of lightning gone astray. The fallen empress set her eyes upon The Night Eye–still very much undead, despite the snake witch's plans to the contrary.

"A serpent's eyes are ever so easy to read–treachery and more treachery," The Night Eye said, approaching at the very tip of the storm. "Are you surprised to see us, snake queen? Your *rulku* cub's blood paints the ocean waters. By now, you must know: there is no escaping the eyes of King Blu. The whale god sees all."

"Aeyra was a monstrosity," Thraxis said. "As are you. If the whale god sees all, then he knows my true intent. I would lay all your bodies out upon the open sea for snakes to feast on."

"Fortunately, *Gola Dwyn* has a wiser queen," The Night Eye said, turning their attention to Xyla. "Forget the machinations of Empress Thraxis. King Blu assures you that *Gola Dwyn* will stay under your rule if you turn over Thraxis and all snake lords for the whale god's justice. Do this, and put down your would-be rebellion, and the water snakes of *Gola Dwyn* will be allowed to renounce *Avrah* and choose the true god of creation, King Blu. Your kingdom will be added to his ocean empire, and all will be forgiven."

"Sweet words," Empress Xyla said, "are often laced with sweet poison. I welcome Thraxis' fall. Take the crazy witch now, if you wish. But what assurance do I have for the lives of my children? Perhaps King Blu means to strike us all. Perhaps the whale god knows that *Gola Dwyn* is not so weak, that we may indeed draw blood from his children before our great fall."

"The assurance is that you still live," The Night Eye said. "No further assurance will be given. The largest navy ever assembled lies just beyond those storm clouds. The immortal shark king Xrata lives. He readies monsters not even Thraxis could have dreamt of, while dragons of undead horrors secure the skies. Surrender now, if you care for the lives of your snake children. If not, King Blu will wipe the jungles and tributaries of all life and turn your kingdom over to the snakes of the sea."

Thraxis struck at Xyla, strangling the empress upon the spot. "I wish I could say you were faithful," Thraxis said, winding herself around the smaller boa constrictor. "Even so, you served your purpose well. Unfortunately for you, there can be only one empress."

Xyla fought to reach Thraxis with a poisoned tongue, but the fallen empress was too calculating. Thraxis threw Xyla's limp body into the sea. The Night Eye looked in disbelief as the second fallen empress of *Gola Dwyn* rolled in the waves before them.

"You should have listened to Xyla's last words more closely," Thraxis said, eying The Night Eye, "Arrogant ravens. I would have loved to let my snakes feast upon you. I hunger to feel the squirming of your helpless bodies as you clawed at my coiled skin. But only now, false prophets, do you see clearly. The nanobots of The Spear Of Black Fire were poisoned, thanks to me. Aeyra didn't need to kill you. He just needed to set the spear free. And the spear has worked its magic, hasn't it, ridding us of your unwanted omens once and for all? I once said there was a poison for everything. I didn't know for sure until I saw the eyes of King Blu. Yours was a slow-acting poison, one of my own devising, with a few enhancements from the skin of the whale god. Even so, you lasted longer than I expected. I marvel that you're able to flutter about at all. I suppose it's true: the hubris of crows knows no bounds."

The Night Eye cackled off the threat until two or three ravens–and then five crows–and then untold kites–fell to the sea. Thraxis hissed a cold, calculating laugh. The ravens convulsed, frothing at the beak, and soon the crows and kites did the same. Blackbirds fell, along with untold legions of spies from the skies. Thraxis watched as the waters sucked up the poison.

"As fortune would have it," Thraxis said, "the poison is also surprisingly effective in water."

Watching The Night Eye fall, King Blu's army held to the sea. There was a battle cry, perhaps from the dragons themselves. The waves thundered in song. Whales breached. The orders were clear. Thraxis's own children, led by the undead Feng himself, swarmed around her.

Holograms of the great snake appeared in the sky, sea, and river. Thraxis hissed her own battle cry. In a moment, holographic images of Qylar The Hunter appeared, surrounded by snakes. His tentacles strangled many until the numbers became too much. Another hologram of King Croc appeared, as the occupying crocodile legions fought against massive numbers of vipers and boas.

Feng signaled. "You cannot fight death and live, Mother," Feng said. "Let our fire cleanse you of life."

Feng roared. The Dragon Guard surrounded Thraxis. Their mouths opened as they became the fire. More fire than burned Zehrah flew over every scale of Thraxis. Yet, Thraxis merely said, "Thank you, my children. You've given me exactly what I needed."

With that, the hologram that was Thraxis disappeared. Where Thraxis was—when exactly she slithered off, or how—no animal could say.

Tyr-Valon

Amazon Rainforest

Mandau crawled around the *sumaumeira* branches, over two-hundred snake tails above the jungle floor. A quick light in the sky—a pulsing red sun—flared, blinding even the stars. Mandau hissed down to banded tree anoles, who brought the message down to the pink iguanas, who brought the message all the way down to the vipers and boas. Birds cackled and whistled. Geckos jumped up and scurried. The entire jungle floor—a slithering skin of pit vipers, green vine snakes, and rainbow boas—came to life. Even the scarlet macaws and harpy eagles alighted, swirling around the skies as the great thinking machines of *Gola Dwyn* ascended.

King Dryga, Igru, and Yanta all looked at the vastness of the rainbow-colored jungle army before them. The animal lords had thought of the Amazon as a river only, rather than an entire web of tributaries, rivers, and jungles that spread over a good deal of the continent. The efficacy of Thraxis' plan became more apparent.

"My empress assures us," Mandau said, "that King Blu means to flood *Gola Dwyn* entirely to give his navy ample waters for attack. Her legions will handle the shores. Empress Thraxis charges your legions with assisting her jungle children with the assault on King Croc and his crocodiles. Follow the lead of the black caiman. Take out as many of King Croc's hybrid monstrosities as you can."

"I never thought I'd see the day when I'd take orders from a snake," King Dryga said, "but on this day, I'm happy to. Let all animals come together and fight!"

The massive king grizzly stood up on his hind legs, roaring to the bear legions. The grizzlies and black bears rose and called out to the polar bears, who, in turn, called out to the big cats. Sun Stalker, scarred but able, stood up and let his lion's roar rival that of the bears. Yanta and her Stampeders trumpeted. Klang Krugal and his apes gibbered. Moon Herald and his wolves howled loudly enough to shake the stars. The snakes hissed. The eagles shrieked. All of Creation shook. Soon, the entire jungle became a wash of noise, of cries, growls, and howls, as animal breeds of all kinds, down to Pale Ghost and the last of his mice, cried out in honor of the basic dignity of all animals.

So loud were the rebel cries that even the crocodiles navigating Snake River took notice. They lifted their eyes from the murky water weeds to see what sounds stabbed even the waters hiding their snouts. The moment their heads rose, the black caiman struck. The war was on.

"There are untold numbers," King Croc's scout, Hrang, declared. "What are your orders, my liege?"

The river snakes, from massive green anacondas to yellow eyelash vipers, did not let up on their assault. Instead, they used the distraction to weave around the waters, lifting up the massive crocodiles, only to take them to the deeper waters and crush them whole. Even King Croc grew wary of the dark waters.

"Keep them fighting until King Blu's forces arrive," King Croc said. "Cry havoc! Let the jaws of every crocodile drip with the blood of *Animus*!"

With King Croc in the lead, the crocodile beasts crawled from the waters onto the open lands. They were half-*rulku*, half-lizard, the blood of the river snakes adorning their scales. King Dryga and Yanta led the charge, pummeling the crocodile beasts into the wet earth. Yet, further crocodile beasts rose up, stabbing with spears at elephants and bears alike. Klang Krugal shrieked. His apes swung through the air. Their massive gorilla arms lifted the beasts up farther into the trees before releasing their crocodile bodies to the river stones below. Some hissed at death. Others stammered, recovering their senses. The

Stampeders charged again, trampling their bodies until a layer of scales covered the jungle floor.

Still, King Croc fought, Hrang at his side, maiming bear and ape alike. Pale Thunder swooped down with his eagles, but King Croc was too powerful, clutching the throats of the eagles and hawks, snapping them, then tossing the birds to the matted jungle below. Ice Giant growled. Hrang attacked, sinking his teeth into the great white polar bear. Ice Giant mauled at the body until he crushed the penetrating skull. Hrang fell lifeless. Ice Giant stood up, his fur red with blood.

"Flee, red bear," King Croc said, "or feel more teeth tearing out your heart."

"This fight ends," Ice Giant said, "with your skull gracing my den on the northern ice."

King Croc lunged. Ice Giant mauled. The power of the gargantuan bear was too much for even the vast power of the king of all crocodiles. King Croc held the great bear's paws, only for Klang Krugal to swoop in from behind. The momentary distraction was enough. King Croc turned to see his newest foe. Ice Giant reached around, lifting the crocodile lord by his head. Ice Giant brought the full weight of his paws down upon King Croc's skull. King Croc lay stunned. Yanta then stormed through, trampling the crocodile lord, smashing his skull.

"Treacherous beast," Ice Giant said. "Was it worth it to strike a deal with the god of death? Where is he now, in your hour of need?"

"My lord is Death, and Death himself smiles upon all this day," King Croc said, between his fading gasps. "Even you are not beyond his bite."

Ice Giant lifted up the dead body, shaking it free of blood and life for all to behold. Seeing their great lord trampled, the crocodiles retreated to the waters. They fought their way through Mandau and the river snakes in full retreat. Anacondas took some foes. River vipers others. Yet, soon, the message was clear: *Tyr-Valon* belonged to the animals of *Animus*.

King Dryga, clearing the last of the crocodiles by the riverbanks, rose up, growling in full triumph.

"Onward," the bear king ordered. "Let no animal rest until the sea drowns in the blood of its master!"

CHAPTER 21

Gola Dwyn

Amazon River Basin

Upon the wings of the wind they flew, great steel beasts that had the agility of an eagle and the firing power of a red spitting cobra. Each became like a rising star, a corona of color that pulsated as Ruth The Lawless and her legions claimed the sky. The animal lords looked up, wondering what, if anything, the great, steely horned eagles might offer in the way of offense to waters so mighty and so dense. Still, even their presence startled the curious squids and octopi, who glanced up over the treacherous waters at the newest predator of the sea.

"Wait for Thraxis' command," Ruth said to the *rulku* warriors. "She has snakes that see into the deep waters."

A holograph of the great snake queen took to the air before the great steel beasts. The transfigured empress, whose white aura of blinding fire danced upon the scales of her green skin and lit her eyes yellow, then red, uncoiled. Rising to her full height, the hologram must have stood the length of a herd of elephants searching through the sparse foliage of the Serengeti plains. Thraxis' presence was, as always, commanding, stirring the coldest of blood in even the warmest hearts of her prey.

"Hold firm," Thraxis said, via transmission, to Ruth's armada. "My flying terror lizards will join you. They will face Admiral Xrata's secret weapon, the latest plague monsters, my brood of dragons. When Feng and the undead Dragon Guard strike back, unleash the toxins. If my magic is right, the curse of the whale god may yet be neutralized."

Within an owl's shriek, Feng appeared, cutting the clouds away with the thrust of his wings. Feng circled with Alazar The Red, Palavir The Purple, and Thrysta The Silver, and Fyvol, the champion of the dragons, waiting to strike. The dragons were the sky. They looked like one body, a giant hydra of endlessly searching eyes, half-lost to the darkness of the sea mists.

"Hold formation," Feng ordered his undead brood. "Our mother seeks to trap us. Let her make the first move, so that we may see what game she plays."

Ruth The Lawless kept her eyes upon the massive dragons. Thraxis was right. Ruth's ships, modified for animal kind, looked like flying metallic thunderbirds that breathed fire. Yet, even Ruth knew, after seeing so much carnage, that the flying machines were no match for a brood the size of this. Feng was by far the most destructive force in the air. His ability to breathe both on land and under-water made him all the more formidable. Ruth would rather divide the brood and overpower one dragon than face such a massive force with mere machines. She waited and commanded her fellow pilots to do likewise.

Cutting through the mists, giant pterodactyls, long thought hunted and killed after The Serpent War, showed the depth of Thraxis' cunning. An entire aerial army, the pterodactyls vastly outnumbered the brood of dragons. Yet, they were smaller and weaker than their mystical foes. The boldness of Thraxis' strategy became clear: this wasn't meant to be a victory. The snake empress wagered everything on the potency of a magic that might not work, and Ruth's life and the lives of the *rulku* hung in the balance. Yet, what choice was there now? Ruth had no better plan, so she buckled down and waited for the signal.

Immediately, the pterodactyls and other pterosaurs struck. It was clear that they moved as one, controlled by the mind of Thraxis.

"Shall we strike?" Pale Ghost, operating one of the ships, asked.

Ruth hesitated until Thraxis' hologram reappeared in miniature before her.

"The Amazon hides a great many things, including my many children," Thraxis said. "Wait for the advantage–then strike. You only get one opportunity at this, or we all die. When you hear my royal hiss, strike quickly and resolutely."

"Agreed," Ruth said, a hint of distrust in the air. "We will wait."

The dragons made short work of the first of the pterosaurs, roasting them until they fell like cooked meat to the waiting sharks below. Yet, the numbers soon proved too formidable a factor. In essence, Empress Thraxis had created a more ancient version of The Night Eye–a hive of flying terror lizards that circled and swarmed until the numbers were too great. The pterosaurs and pterodactyls did their part, swarming and separating the dragons just enough to temporarily neutralize their power.

Thraxis' hiss took to the air, shaking the clouds and even the flying steel beasts themselves.

"Strike," Ruth ordered. "Make sure every dragon is covered in toxins."

Ruth's ships swarmed The Dragon Guard. Like a spitting cobra, they unleashed their venom with ruthless efficacy. Fyvol, Alazar, Thrysta, and even Palavir writhed in the air before falling to the ocean. Yet, the *rulku* struck one flap of a hummingbird's wings too fast. Feng, only half-covered in toxins, stirred the mighty flames within. The dragon emperor circled back towards the ships and unleashed a black, unearthly fire that enveloped the *rulku* ships and sent them crashing. Ruth and her pilots fought to avoid enemy waters, steering their ships towards the serpentine city lands.

"If anyone is alive to hear," Ruth said. "Get out of the ships immediately! Get ready to fight!"

The *rulku* did as commanded. Yet, Feng, a giant, endless span of wings, pounced upon them, unleashing more black fire. Ruth and the *rulku* that were able rolled out of the way. Pale Ghost, Death Claw, and other animal pilots did the same, only quicker. All waited on Thraxis, hoping the empress might save them. Yet, Thraxis delayed. All Ruth could think of was that Thraxis saw the opportunity to rid herself of more than meddlesome dragons.

"Use my ship as cover," Ruth said.

The *rulku* and animal pilots did as commanded, if only to save their lives. They rolled half of the fractured steel belly of the ship over to absorb the flames. They then ran and hid beside the other half of the ship.

"No," Ruth said, correcting the animals and *rulku*. "Run towards the city."

"We'll never make it," Pale Ghost said as Feng's fire struck the ground around them. "And I am out of portaling magic."

"I will run first," Ruth said. "Follow me this one last time–not to death, but to glory. If there's one thing I've learned from a snake, it's that sometimes slithering away is the smartest move an animal can make. If we're in Thraxis' city, she'll be forced to defend her own or look like a coward before her snakes. To win over a snake, one must first think like a snake."

"It's suicide," Death Claw said.

"Only for me," Ruth said. "When the fire strikes me, don't look back. Keep flying. Keep running. My shoulders have been broad and strong for so very, very long. When they fall, the survival of the animal world falls upon your shoulders. Let your shoulders be strong–for all animals, *rulku* and snake alike. And if he lives, if he ever comes back to himself, tell my son that his warm-blooded mother loved him with enough fire that it would have burned away all his hurt, had it been possible."

Ruth broke free, shrieking a battle cry at the top of her *rulku* lungs. Feng immediately turned upon the *rulku* queen, gathering yet more of his black, undead fire. All around the dragon lord, the undead fire burned beyond when all nature fire became ember and ash. Yet, there was enough room for the mice to crawl through, for the hawks and eagles to fly over, for the smallest of *rulku* to run. Crawl, fly, and run, they did.

Ruth screamed an honorable cry, facing death like a warrior ready to strike. She became a mass of blackened flame, her flesh joining in the darkness as her cry haunted the skies. Pale Ghost and his mice made it clearly through the flame, as did the tiny *rulku* and Death Claw and the hawks and eagles in his company. Thraxis had no choice. She appeared behind her son, whose serpentine sense got the better of him. Feng turned around to greet his mother.

"You gave me life," Feng said. "It is only fair that I give you death in return."

As Feng spoke, Thraxis sprayed the last of the toxin from her massive mouth. Feng writhed, his undead white eyes turning purple, then white again. Feng rose to lunge after Thraxis when The Dragon Guard, led by Fyvol, flew to him, holding their dragon emperor to the ground. Thraxis watched as Feng regained his sense of self.

"How do you feel?" Thraxis asked her son.

"Like the whale god swam in and swallowed my soul, only to set it free again," Feng said.

The dragon emperor looked around him. The pterosaurs lifted up their cry.

"King Blu set nothing free," Thraxis said. "I did. And I tell you now, these animal creatures are your allies. Fight with us, or the world, lizards and *rulku* alike, will be lost."

Feng roared, a fresh fire bristling along his fangs. "King Blu wanted these dragon wings to be his agent of death from the air," Feng said. "He may get his wish. Come, dragon warriors. Let us show the orca and shark lords the true meaning of dragon fire."

With that, Feng and The Dragon Guard rose to the air, and The Army of The Black Ocean shrunk just a little more into unseen waters.

No Rul Ozu

Inyo County, California, USA

King Blu swam in time and before time, all at once. The great leviathan, the first of all whales, saw just how much *Avrah* had deceived his senses, slumbering these many millennia as they were. The great goddess was indeed the fabled Tree Of Life, *Yggdrasil,* her roots extending to the soils of the earth, her branches pollinating untold families of trees, ferns, and flowers, each extending, in roots that took on the shape of the earth, into the very belly of Creation. Whereas King Blu's children grew downward, into the crevices of molten rock, *Avrah's* children grew towards the sky, into the farthest heights that trees had stood or that birds had flown. Yet, even as King Blu stirred the sea to fury, he wondered, somewhere where fears come alive and gnaw at the heart, whether he had underestimated the sheer scope of *Avrah*. The last time god and goddess came face to face, a world was born. This time, King Blu reasoned, the world would fall.

Yet, there was something that stood against reason, which stood as tall as the millennia that stood between—the witchy trees, seers with no eyes, sisters of strange seed, planted in Time itself. They joined in the web of roots uniting the world, facing the lone sea. King Blu could hear their voices as if they emanated from the crustaceans crawling directly beneath him. Indeed, *Avrah* was present in all things.

"A black heart rises in the ocean," Methuselah said, her branches swaying in the fire winds. "The whale god has come."

"I sense a certain something—do you, sisters?" The Mystic called out. "Eyes of fire, wrapped within a flaming globe."

"I feel…fury," Lady Diurnia said, "a stirring black hole turned in upon itself. It swirls and twirls, a storm eating a storm within a storm until the world is no more."

"I see the storm, sister—a massive, black-striped body of blue fire, neither orca nor blue whale nor monstrous leviathan, yet father of all three."

"The whale god comes to set eyes upon his mirror goddess, the firstborn of Creation," Old Tijikko said. "He may not like what he sees."

"He has a bloody purpose—but there is no blood in trees," Lama said. "Only roots that run deep as sea upon sea."

"Yet, the tides of time have at last caught us, sisters. As one wave falls, another rises,"

King Clone added.

"Send our sentinel to guide him through strange waters," Jumon Sugi commanded, "to even stranger destiny."

"The Firebird must go," Pando said. "Let the god of the sea follow the divine fire. Let the promised sign herald the end times."

In a moment, fire cracked against the sky and the phoenix-like thunderbird of fire, Nurvlyn, Zehrah, the ancient acolyte, The Firebird, sprung forth. His wings lit the clouds as he buffeted them, heading out into the billowing ocean that, like a great tsunami, wound around the desert sands of *No Rul Ozu*.

"Call back the golden mists, sisters," Methuselah said. "When the tip of the firebird's wings lights them, the battle of wills begins."

King Blu, still circling and billowing the great tides until they inched closer and closer into the desert, rested for a moment to see the work of an angry god. The waters rose higher than in any time since before the *rulku* walked upon *Avrah's* earthly body. Mountains upon mountains of water swelled, rising to wash out the sun itself before crashing into the desert sands below. Soon, King Blu would be face to face with *Avrah* for the first time since tetrapods crawled out of the ocean waters so many sun cycles ago.

Just then, King Blu sensed something. The whole sky became like wings of fire. Even from the depths, he could sense the presence of The Firebird. The whale god breached the waters long enough to see the otherworldly wings beckoning him forward. The manner of the bird–unrepentant fire–burned into the whale god's mind. This wasn't a welcome. This was a challenge.

"Nurvlyn," King Blu said. "The lost prophet, not quite *rulku,* not quite beast. It seems you've found your sacred place after all."

"As will we all, whale god," The Firebird said without saying. "As will you, when you join with Creation."

"So, you are a bird of warning," King Blu said. "Very well, then. Lead on, Firebird. I shall follow. There is no trap lethal enough to ensnare the god of death."

King Blu saw, only too late, the wisdom of *Avrah.* As The Firebird lit the way through the skies, the clouds grew like rolling thunder incarnate. King Blu saw that the great fire blasts of gold and black held not just flame but the very embodiment of *Avrah.* The sinewy, winding roots of The Great Tree Of Life, Methuselah herself, wound throughout the core husk of the world, branching out to every conceivable plant, to every conceivable creature. Even the largest of whales who had fed on plankton had *Avrah* within them. *Avrah* was here, hidden in the desert waste before the great whale god. Yet, *Avrah* was everywhere else too. King Blu realized that the sheer scope of *Avrah's* growth and omnipresence was why he failed to recognize his godly twin. To recognize *Avrah* was to recognize part of himself.

"Greetings, Brother Sea," Methuselah sang, in a song not unlike whale song teeming in the black depths of endless water. "How I have missed you."

The waters rose, lifting the whale god, until the crests of fortune brought him face to face with The Witchy Sisters, the great roots of *Avrah* in the known world. The holograms of the witches spread from Methuselah, as if part of a larger Tree Of Life covering the whole of the earth.

"Yes, welcome," Pando said, radiating in yellow light, "spirit of my spirit."

"And darkness to my light," The Mystic said, beaming in majestic purple.

"Welcome, time and the timeless," Old Tijikko added, iridescent.

"Ancient god, welcome," Lama said, burning in a nourishing orange fire.

"Challenger, who shall also be challenged, speak," Lady Diurnia said.

"Speak, and determine the fate of the earth," Jumon Sugi said, in completion.

"Speak. Let your words be your herald; let your song be your fire," King Clone said, in admonition.

King Blu took in the full scope of *Avrah*, saw the roots and the children of the sky that saw all. Not one speck of soil, not one blade of grass, not one seed in the sky, was not the fruit of *Avrah*.

King Blu rose, breaching the tallest of the waves, as he chanted his song of death. It was not a harsh song–cold, cacophonous, detached. It was a song of fiery, rhythmic cadences that rose from the farthest corners of Creation–like the downy barbs of the gentlest white feather gliding through the virgin summer air. Yet, in the song was the whole of King Blu. There were the first moments when King Blu understood that he was ocean and not ocean all at once; there was the time he floated through the skies as a single-celled organism, the first seed falling into the waters of life. There was a cry of what had happened to waters that for millions of sun cycles had followed the same currents–millions of whale births, long, fruitful lives with mates and calves and new songs, all coalescing into a single song of the great whale kingdom, of the ocean itself. King Blu's heart was the keeper of that song. How beautiful that song was, and then, in a single undulation, how ghastly. The song of the last thousands of years of sun cycles was a dark one, all about the rise of the *rulku,* the harpooning of mothers, the poisoning of waters, the treachery of Azaz–a cry of accusation, a call for blood. The notes of the whale song, a celebration and a lament, fell like an ice so frigid it burned the branches of Methuselah and her sisters with its lament.

"My song rages," King Blu said, "not in fire, but in blood. Every whale that has ever been cries out for justice. Every sea particle that has been raped and ravaged calls out for the blood of the animal race. It is time to clean the earth of its cancers. It is time for The Great Miscreation to unfold."

In answer to the cry came the great chastisement. Not since the first collective growl of the animal kingdom levied against the usurping powers of the *rulku* had a song cried out in such lethal might. King Blu's song, reverberating throughout air and land, shook all of Creation. Not one flying fowl did not feel a tremor in her wings. Not one slithering snake did not feel the cold rock of earth stabbing into its belly. Not one running hoof did not tremble, shake, and shatter, as thousands upon thousands of animals fell to the earth and sea, killed by the song that once gave them life.

"Stop," Methuselah and her sisters commanded.

The earth froze; the song, which wove through the golden mists, tearing them apart with slithering black shadow, froze as well.

"Now," Methuselah said. "Hear our song."

CHAPTER 22

Gola Dwyn
Amazon River Basin

A wave of fire, like some misshapen hell, stood between sky and sea. Feng and The Dragon Guard breathed their full fury into the ocean waters. The bubbling steam became like glassy shards of fire. Still, the bodies fell everywhere. Fowl, otters, snakes, and bears–none were immune to the great deathly cry of King Blu. As if it were an omen, Admiral Xrata arched his back, signaling his great white troops to circle the periphery of the fires. The massive great white sharks, blue whales, and killer orcas stirred the waters. Fires fell to the feasting ocean. The bull sharks, enraged, led the charge. The massive sea bulls pressed at the waiting vipers, slicing them in two. Alazar The Red blew reams of bloody flame at King Blu's champion. Yet, Admiral Xrata swam ahead, biting at the leg of the red dragon until Alazar was forced to retreat. Despite Thraxis' newest aerial force, The Army of The Black Ocean sounded the battle cry of a full advance.

"The time is now. Press our full numbers into every tributary surrounding *Gola Dwyn*," Admiral Xrata ordered. "Lay siege. Before night, the tower of the empress must fall."

Thraxis was not alone on The Throne Tower when Admiral Xrata's cry reached her ears. So vicious, so thunderous was the silent cry of the mighty sharks that even the most towering of the anacondas turned to her, as if to ask, *Are you sure? Is this the day we die?* Thraxis' eyes held no answer. The great serpent queen knew on this day, the foundations of everything *Animus Sur* stood for would be razed. The heart of the animal world would be tested like never before. Still, the aged empress knew that her snakes were nothing if not the heart of the fight.

"Let them fill in their greater numbers," Thraxis commanded. "If you can't bring The Trojan Horse into the city, then you can make the city The Trojan Horse."

"Empress?" Mandau asked.

"It's an old *rulku* expression," Thraxis explained. "When King Blu's eyes searched the seas for *Avrah*, I had a search of my own. I found something quite special: King Blu's lair. Shards of a true crown, forged by servants of King Blu himself. Before the day is done, the ocean will feel its power."

Fill the waters the sharks, eels, dolphins, and whales did–in hellacious numbers. Admiral Xrata ordered the giant squids to the mouths of the rivers. The whales burst through any bombardment of snakes, impenetrable to the venom of their bites. The sleekest of sharks, among them the blacktip reef sharks and the pugnacious bull sharks, assailed the rivers. They fought everything. Shark legions feasted on any fish or snakes that got in the way, even the swarming piranhas.

All this Thraxis watched from her tower, even as her snakes cried for mercy.

"Do we strike, empress?" Mandau asked.

"We wish to save as many snakes as possible. Order the animal lords to advance to the city," Thraxis ordered. "Once they do, release the nanotoxins into the waters."

"Will not our own snakes die, my empress?" Mandau asked in reply.

"A few–so that many more may live. Death takes a bite from every meal, commander," Thraxis said. "But these nanobots are special." Thraxis arched her back, as if marveling at her own ingenuity. "They are from the whale god himself. He forgets that I see his mind as he sees mine. These nanobots will kill some valiant snake lords–that is true. But they will kill far more of King Blu's children. For the golden blue nanobots are conditioned to attack anything at all that disturbs the whale god's lair. The whales, sharks, and dolphins, in particular, will be seen as aggressors."

Mandau hissed half-approvingly. "The whale god is clever above all else," Mandau said. "Will he not suspect?"

As Mandau formulated her words, a serpentine smile formed from the fangs of her empress.

"That's the point, isn't it, my empress?" Mandau asked, in answer to her own question. "The whale god either has to give his full attention to the assault on *Gola Dwyn* or on the tree witches. Even King Blu cannot do both."

"Even a god has his limits," Thraxis said. "Once you order the animal lords to the city, order Aeyra to the ocean waters behind the giant squids. Tell him that it is time he puts his bond with the whale god to use."

The snake lord Mandau looked at her ruthless empress with renewed reverence. She could see that Thraxis had planned for this very moment for the better part of a generation, from when her thunderbirds first plucked the *rulku* cub from his mother. Yet, the whale god had swum the ocean for eons, before Thraxis even burst from her egg. To match wits with a god was a very dangerous game indeed.

Mandau complied, using the holo ether to appear before the animal lords.

"King Dryga," Mandau said.

The king of bears had fangs full of the blood of crocodiles.

"I see you've been hunting," Mandau said. "My empress requests that you reinforce her snakes in the heart of *Gola Dwyn*. The sharks, whales, and dolphins swarm our waters. They seek to take down The Throne Tower and, with it, *Animus Sur*."

"I remember watching the spirit of Azaz face King Blu," King Dryga said. "I remember watching Azaz fall and with him, *Animus Nor*–all so that I might live. I have lost one kingdom to the whale god. I will not lose another."

King Dryga rose to his full height, swatches of blood adorning the fur of his haunches. Yanta trumpeted. Sun Stalker roared. Pale Thunder shrieked a bloody admonition to the harbingers of the skies. The Army of The Black Ocean would rise to face the jewel of *Animus Sur*, and the animal lords would be there to meet them.

Mandau searched out the nanosphere for the *rulku* wizard, but Aeyra was silent. Only when Mandau searched the nanorobotic signatures of the deep waters did he see the gilled *rulku* just floating just beyond the army's reach.

"Master Aeyra," Mandau said. "Your mother calls you. She says it's time to use the power your brush with the whale god has given you."

"My mother is dead," Aeyra said, contemplating Ruth's last stand. "Once, I might have asked which mother that was. Now, I know. It's not one mother. It's two. And the same fate has come for both. I can do what the snake empress commands. But the power she seeks to harness is beyond all control. The whale god's eyes touched me with a destiny darker than a sunless ocean frozen in Arctic night. Anything in my path will die."

Cold-blooded as Mandau was, even she grimaced at the abomination before her. Yet, the servant had little choice but to trust the master.

"Thraxis assures me," Mandau said, after a moment's hesitation, "that if there's ever a time, it's now. Admiral Xrata moves his forces. King Blu's armies mean to take the city by nightfall."

"I am a curse to the world, like my father before me," Aeyra said. "Let that curse fall where it may."

Mandau nodded in assent. The snake lord's hologram vanished. The ocean shook. Even Aeyra felt the pulsing of the sea. Admiral Xrata ordered his grand assault. The monsters of the darkest depths of the ocean would soon be upon

Animus Sur. Yanta and King Dryga positioned themselves just beyond the crashing waves. Klang Krugal climbed the outer wall of The Throne Tower, calling for his ape armies to do the same. Moon Herald and the wolves kept with the bears, tearing at any reef sharks that neared the edge of the waters. Pale Thunder and Blood Talon struck the sky and sea, assaulting the thunderbirds. The fighting bloodied sky, land, and sea. A roar—grating, bellowing, and agonizing—announced the arrival of the terror lizards. King Blu, the master of plagues, had yet to unleash the last of his monsters. These were multiple plagues, dragons of his own design, standing from sea to sky, with pairs of black wings and red, searing eyes. Feng and The Dragon Guard swooped in. But even the son of Thraxis knew that such dragons were larger and mightier than he was.

"The last Plague Monsters rise from the depths," Admiral Xrata cried out. "Our time is at hand. Full assault! Let every shark take a bite of Creation!"

Above the great white shark king, in The Throne Tower, Thraxis perceived the latest turn in the battle differently. "Release the blue nanobots—now," Thraxis ordered Mandau. "Anything from the sea should buckle under the pestilence of the whale god."

Thraxis' plague bots swept the ocean waters furiously. The animal lords watched in terror as the sharks, dolphins, and whales writhed. The elegant sea beasts squirmed until the bots raced through their bodies, leaving them to bleed into the sea. Poison from the blue nanobots was such that blinded shark turned upon blinded shark, that whale attacked whale. Several orcas and dolphin pods maimed themselves tearing blooms of giant jellyfish apart. The giant squids fought to stop the monstrous lords from killing each other. Yet, even they were not immune, their tentacles writhing, then falling still.

At first, Fire Hoof made a great clicking cry. Igru rose up, mooing mightily. Victory seemed at hand.

But the power of King Blu could be felt even from the farthest seas. His song had not just sent out a deathly cry that decimated at least one-third of the animals in Creation. The whale god had sent a fresh golden plague cloud back upon the kingdom of *Animus Sur* with his deathly song. The animals caught sight of it as bird upon bird fell to the bloodied waters.

"Back to The Throne Tower," Yanta ordered.

The animals—not just elephants but bears, wolves, oxen, and snakes—heeded the cry. Yet, for any of the slower, plodding polar bears, the golden cloud was too much. The poison overtook them—even Ice Giant, who fought to guide the polar bear young ahead of him.

"Thraxis' tower," Klang Krugal cried out. "It's locked!"

Pale Ghost and his mice ate at the locks, but there was too little time. Old as he was, the foremost mind of *Animus Nor* lost his balance. His great-great-grand-children reached for him, but the wisest mouse to ever live freed their paws from his.

"Go, my children," Pale Ghost said. "Life has wrapped me in its fire and set me ablaze. My fire is yours now. Take that fire and blaze brightly."

Upon his last words, Pale Ghost fell and perished in the sea below.

The animals let up their cry–for Ice Giant, for Pale Ghost, for all the name-less dead–but there was no time to mourn. Visible from a closed window stood Empress Thraxis herself. Whether she knew of King Blu's backlash or not, the serpentine smile never left her fangs. This would be her chance to take over the animal world–or what was left of it–after her great fall at the eyes of King Blu. Not only the animals of the sea would fall, but every animal lord from every warring continent–all in one deadly swipe of fortune's blade. The world–such as it was–would be hers. Thraxis contemplated this–what she wanted most in all the world, nothing less than the world–with a vacant smile.

"My empress," Mandau said. "In a moment, the animal lords will all be dead."

"To be the living empress of a dead world," Thraxis said, "or to be the dead empress of a living world? Such a cruel irony–is it not, Mandau? To have ev-erything I wanted handed to me by the very Fates that cast me down. It is a tempting question for any queen to consider–is it not? Yet, I know the answer. It is the answer of any true empress. Place the crown upon my head. Let *Avrah* do what she will."

"Are you sure, my empress?" Mandau asked. "To make an enemy of one god is folly. To make an enemy of two gods is suicide."

"I am at war only with myself, Mandau," Thraxis said. "Today, that war is over. Signal Aeyra. His time is here."

Mandau did so as the apes fought to smash the tower windows.

Thraxis slithered over, opening the windows. She ordered every window open throughout the tower. Klang Krugal swung in, as did his apes.

Thraxis turned to Klang Krugal and said, "The crown I wear now can only be worn by King Blu. Only two land animals have looked into the eyes of the whale god and lived. I am one. Aeyra is the other. What I start, only Aeyra can finish." Thraxis hissed, calling forth a breath to force out the last of her words. "Do not touch me, or you will surely die. Aeyra must take the crown. There is no other way for our world to survive. Flee the tower when you see the great fire."

Klang Krugal's eyes filled with all kinds of emotions as he contemplated the snake empress anew. "I died once," Klang Krugal said. "There is darkness, but there is also light."

"Don't mistake this for heroics," Thraxis said. "In another age, I would have killed you all without the slightest hesitation. In this age, in this time–this is the only way. Such is the life of a snake–a series of twists and turns along a road that never stops winding."

Mandau called out, "Brace yourselves. Don't be directly in front of Empress Thraxis. Flee if you wish to save your lives!"

With that, the snake lord placed the crown of the whale upon the head of the snake. A light to banish all lights–at once white, black, opaque, impenetrable, ungodly, and unyielding–sprang from the crown. The blinding fire of light came alive, running towards the poisoned golden mists. Light twisted and turned, shrieking, like three banshees breaking off and tearing from the clouds. Wild light dissolved the great mists of the whale god and grew hungrier still. Admiral Xrata ordered his elite terror lizards to strike, but Feng's aerial army held them at bay. The light struck relentlessly into the heart of the ocean. Aeyra, poised by the last of the giant squids, seized the light. It took hold of his eyes. The *rulku* abomination magnified the light, releasing it in a dreadful cry. Aeyra unleashed the light upon Admiral Xrata himself. Light blazed through the king of the sharks, burning the blackness of his undead form. The king of the great white sharks writhed, fighting to tear Aeyra apart. The light held King Blu's champion, until he was no more than a river of ash floating upon a bloody sea. Aeyra sent another banshee of light towards The Plague Monsters. The light turned the abominations to ashes where they stood.

Thraxis cried out as the weight of the light consumed her. The high queen shrank and fell. The Throne Tower shook under her massive weight.

Aeyra took the last of Thraxis' light. Raising and extending his arms, the *rulku* beast magnified the light in all directions until it became like an underwater sun. Whales, sharks, dolphins, octopi, and eels swarmed after the unholy light harbinger. Aeyra stretched his arms again, parting the light. The lords of the sea burst through, lunging after Aeyra. Aeyra then let the light flood through the waters, burning the mighty creatures to ash.

The crown of the whale god, the one true crown of the animals, fell from Thraxis into the sea. Aeyra seized the crown. The animal lords, those of land and sea, watched. Aeyra smirked as he thought of the power in his hands. Yet, he knew what he must do. Only one act would stir the attention of the whale god. Only one act would save *Avrah*. Aeyra took The Spear Of Black Fire in hand and brought its full weight upon the crown. The crown smashed into several scarring fires. Aeyra felt the full heat of the whale god's fire. He reached out, the voice of Fowler overtaking him, as he buried the fires beneath the deepest recesses of the sea–and was seen no more.

The tower fell–and with it, Thraxis–burned through by the light. The animal lords fled towards the Amazonian jungle. Shaking the land was not just the light. The death cry of King Blu, so distant and so near, thundered through the fires. Some animals swore there were words in the whale song–words of passing, words of peace. Others swore there was a curse wrapped in the whale song, a promise that death should never be banished from the world. Each animal heard the voice of the whale god in a unique and striking way. With that, The Armies of the Black Ocean fled. The battle was over. Only the light–shining, deadly, transformative–remained.

No Rul Ozu
Inyo County, California, USA

King Blu's song of death hung frozen in the air. The whale god swam in circles, ushering in cataclysmic waves. Yet, the Witchy Sisters held land, sky, and sea in a trance. Their golden mists blinded even the all-seeing eyes of the whale god himself.

And then the wind sang. The song started with the gentlest of notes, that heralding of the first drop of water in the first ocean. Methuselah and her sisters called up images of the heroic pageantry of life. There was the first molecule–clear, translucent, miraculous–hovering before hitting the next molecule, starting the chain reaction that would bring life to lifeless rock. Even the rock itself turned into music, as nothing was without life. The molecules became increasingly complex algae blooming until wondrous creations like liverworts and mosses took hold of the rock. From those smallest of plants grew the sweeping grasses and the tallest of trees, from the roots of Pando to the immortal presence of Methuselah herself. And it wasn't just the plants–*Avrah* became so many forms, from the first cry of the arthropods to the last cry of the tyrannosaurus rex. From the first sea horse to the first dragonfly, from the first flowering plant to the gardens of lost Eden–all was *Avrah*. In all of this were the mighty sharks, the ancient whales, the fearless eagles, and the predatory owls. Nature became one pulse, one continuous and ever-beating heart. Even after one mass extinction and then another and another, life found a way. Life always found a way. And as The Mystic's branches danced, as Pando sung with the wind, as Lady Diurnia and Old Tijikko and Lama offered a chorus to Methuselah's wondrous song, there was an image of the smallest molecules that would form the body of King Blu assembling. There was an image of the molecules breaking off and forming countless other lifeforms, like the algae of the ocean, like the albatross falling into the sea. King Blu saw his molecules join on the land too, forming the mother of wolves and the father of bears. The song was so complete, so full of vibrancy, that for a moment even the whale god swam in awe.

"It's a song without a beginning, a middle, or an end," Methuselah said. "The song was me, and I was you. We are all different notes of the same eternal song. *Avrah* is King Blu and King Blu is *Avrah,* not as brother and sister, so much as one and same god forgetting, then remembering."

"These children are you–" Old Tijikko added.

"–And you are them," Lama said.

"In a song that will never end," Lady Diurnia and The Mystic sang in chorus.

"There is no death, only rebirth, only the great becoming of all that is," Methuselah added. "And so now, King Blu, heart of my heart, soul of my soul, he whose journey has been so long–rest in my song."

Just then, King Blu felt the crown of crowns shattering. His eyes fell on Thraxis and Aeyra, not as foes to crush into ungodly waters, but as children, as his children, as much a part of him as he was of the ocean that bred him.

"It is so…beautiful," the whale god sang, lost in awe. "I had forgotten. I am tired, so very, very tired. My heart is full. My soul is ready."

Methuselah released her golden clouds, the very same that skirted across the skies of the earth, from the waters of *Ku-Rah* to the river city of *Gola Dwyn.*

In a shadowy fire of gold and black, in the magic of Snow Prophet, Freyda, Criddock, and the trees, the animal lords emerged. They stood wrapped in the flames of the same eternal song. There was Moon Shadow, in blazing white glory, her snout raised as she, Sun Shadow and their pups howled in welcome. There was White Claw, standing with Azaz and Ice Giant, the three bears growling in homage. There were Thunder Killer and Sky Death, flying in tribute with The Night Eye around the sky and sea and all that was. And there was Pale Ghost, bowing, near Yorba and Zulta, who trumpeted in honor of the king of all animals. Xrata and Silver Snake swam in greeting. Groth The Impaler hissed. Dasu growled. The Firebird that was Nurvlyn lit the sky afire and Fowler after him. Lastly, Thraxis came slithering forward, hissing in triumph, completing the tail of the great shadow fire.

With that, the whale god let up a great cry–not of wrath, but of celebration for the life and death and life that always would be, that always was.

It is said that, at that moment, King Blu passed from this world. Yet, a god never dies. Some sparrows say King Blu became the sea. Some lions say that he became the swimming stars, giving light to the dark waters of space. Still, the most ancient of owls say he became the mighty song that even the smallest of animals hears in the dead of night–the song that binds Creation. Whatever King Blu was, whatever he became, he was, in the end, what he was in the beginning–as unfathomable, as miraculous, as terrifyingly beautiful as life itself.

CHAPTER 23

Gola Dwyn

The Amazon Rainforest

Snow Prophet circled the air in a world reborn. Below, the animal lords ambled towards their victory *blot*. There walked King Dryga and his Blood Paw guards, speaking with Feng and the dragon lords. Pale Thunder and Death Talon flew above them, heralding the animal lords to come and celebrate peace. Yanta and Klang Krugal walked by the bonfires, conversing like friends turned enemies turned friends. Each animal knew that the world would never bear the same winds again. They kept the passing of Pale Ghost–and of all their animal friends–in every unspoken thought. As the winds swept them, the animal lords knew: the animal tribes would integrate and the old *Animus* would be like a Tower of Babel, a legend without skin, lost to Time. New worlds would be built with representatives from all animals of all tribes. The first animals to be awakened by the ravages of fortune would be like shadows of a forgotten sun. Names like Moon Shadow, Thraxis, and Azaz would be temple gods, stars of their own constellations. Their tales would be so old that even the most wizened of animals would assume they were the legends of graybeards, animals who never roamed the earth at all. Generations later, the snake scholars would argue that the first animal lords were merely conflated phantoms of a shadowy past, legends without legs, no more real than the alleged *rulku* cities once said to dot the earth.

But in his circling, Snow Prophet felt something of a vision lifting his ancient wings. The old owl priest could see the feasting animal lords looking below him, towards a field between jungles, where animals roamed freely. These were not awakened animals, like Sky Death all those suns ago. They were pure, innocent *Criollo*, gelding and stallion alike, as much a part of nature as the first hoof to pound against the first rock. Snow Prophet, like so many animal prophets doomed to live past his time, looked down upon the beautiful beasts, not without longing. They were tall and sturdy, with delicate earth-brown fur and starless black tails. Majestic and broad-shouldered, the *Criollo* beasts ran at full might, as if the entire band might stampede a pink-black horizon that seemed to never end. How careless the strange, naked creatures looked–how wild, reckless, and free–never having seen a war, never having been hunted by *rulku* seeking only domination. Snow Prophet saw the light in King Dryga's eyes, in the eyes of all the animal lords. They were a world apart now. There was no going back to the cradle of nature that once suckled them. In those eyes was the pain of all knowledge, the agonizing paradox of being a part of the natural world and standing apart from it all at once.

This must be how Man felt, Snow Prophet thought, *when He first emerged from the caves.*

For a brief moment, Snow Prophet thought of the first raindrop to ever fall upon the first leaf. How impossibly beautiful nature was–how sacred and savage, how pure and unfathomable, how illustriously light and how profoundly dark. There were so many tales, so many animals, trees, microbes even, over countless eons, lost to the sieve-like hands of Time–the greatest of all creatures to have ever lived, never to be seen again. The noblest of all animals were now dead and mute before the greatest predator of all–cold, unfeeling Time itself. Would this age of the animal be any different? Who would there be to honor this age, to sing of its lost heroes, to remember the exact moment when a blade of grass first broke the barren rock? To know when the first river flowed into the primordial ocean, creating–against all odds–the resiliency of life? *There will come a time,* Snow Prophet thought. *There will come a time. Every wing that soars falters; every leg that runs upon the earth one day becomes it. What falls, rises. What rises, falls. The future is the past is the future.*

EPILOGUE

Life and death are two winds that blow over the same sea—so Snow Prophet finished scrawling on The Holy Tablets. *One speaks gently, the other harshly, but if you listen long enough, they become one and the same breeze. So it was in The Great War of the Sea, when gods became animals and animals became gods. The whispers of glory still haunt the winds, for any animals that care to listen. Burn brightly, brothers and sisters, the whispers tell us, for every sun that rises—like King Blu, the great black sun of the ocean—shall one day burn no more, and every star that lights the night sky shall die in the light of a new day. This is the way of the earth—of the land, sea, and sky. This is the way of the animal. Cherish the day; revel in the night. Let the sacred burn through you. Let the fire of life never die.*

From *War of the Animals book 4: Azaz, King of Kings*

CHAPTER 1

Gungsung Dor
Rockies, USA

There is one moment that shaped the great king of the fire bears above all others. Once, when he was a tiny cub of black and brown fury, an unnamed bear saw hunters on the mountain as he foraged with his mother. The bear had a heart of fire, but the fire in those days burned for knowledge and love. The cub enjoyed exploring, roaming along river and creek, sticking its snout into whatever cluster of white yarrow spotted the slope. For a single sun cycle, the bear was content with flower, rock, and sun. That's when *Adyre,* in bear tongue, or Gentle River, locked eyes with his first *rulku.* Most animals remember the experience in the days just after the end of days: the moment their eyes spot a strange predator that does not follow *Ozu,* who hunts to kill like a rabies-ridden mongrel. It is the moment most animals first learn fear. And so, it was with *Adyre* when he spotted the *rulku* hunters between his mother and him. The fear was uncontrollable, like the raging river spilling over into night. *Adyre,* though yet a cub, stood up on his hind legs. He sniffed, huffed, growled. The two *rulku* stopped. At first they seemed *sylarg,* consumed with the water that makes *rulku* crazy. They stumbled about, laughing at the sight. Yet, in his heart, *Adyre* made a promise. *Be gone,* he had said in the bear tongue of old, *or I will kill you.* Before the final growl, *Adyre's* mother rose to her full height.

"Look at the size of that one," one *rulku* said to the other. "Easy, girl! We're just hunting elk. Back off!"

The first *rulku* tried to make itself bigger, screaming and waving a thunder-stick.

The second *rulku* shook its head and said, "That's a grizzly. You don't fight a grizzly, you stupid drunk! You shoot her dead or you end up dead yourself!"

The first *rulku* stood for a second with the eyes of death upon him.

That look was all it took. *Myrgle,* or Winter Blood, as the cub's mother was named, mauled the *rulku* with steel thunder in his hands. The *rulku,* too water-crazy to balance his thunderstick, fell over. Within a crack of mountain thunder, Winter Blood was upon him. The mother grizzly mauled at his neck as the *rulku* screamed, fighting to cover himself. Claws draped in skin emerged, only to sink into flesh again. The second *rulku* grabbed the thunderstick. Gentle River stood on his hind legs again, crying out. The *rulku* killer ignored the cub. He aimed the thunderstick right at Winter Blood's head. She lifted her head from her first victim, turning it slightly, just in time to see the mortal blow. One crack of thunder. Then another. Gentle River growled in agony. Winter Blood fell. Gentle River ran to poke his snout at his mother. She lay still, blood matting the front of her head. Gentle River looked in Winter Blood's eyes, but the fire bear had already come. Winter Blood was gone, a shadow of flame searching out a distant sun.

"Are you all right?" the first *rulku* cried to the other.

"My face! My neck!" the fallen *rulku* screamed. "Get something for the blood!"

Gentle River watched as one *rulku* attended to ripping off part of his shirt and bandaging the head and neck wounds of his fallen friend. The thunderstick fell to the ground, right by Winter Blood's reddening body.

"Go on–get! Move! Get out of here, stupid bear!" the second *rulku* said as he bandaged the first one. "Go–or end up just like your mother!"

There was something in the tone of the *rulku,* something in the pointing gesture, in the finger nearly jerking low enough to hit his mother's corpse, that killed the gentleness in *Adyre* that day on the mountain. Reckless *rulku* had taken blood but felt no need to repay with blood of their own. The cub, though small, did something in that moment that no other cub in the grizzly clans of *Gungsung Dor* had ever done. He attacked, using his weight to push the second *rulku* off of the first. The second *rulku* yelled as he toppled. The first *rulku* reached for the thunderstick. His drunken hand took the gun, pressed upon the trigger. *Adyre* moved. The bullet lodged right in the head of the first drunken *rulku,* who was busy scrambling to his feet before taking the bullet right in the skull and sinking to the earth below. The fallen first *rulku,* seeing what he had done, screamed.

"You're dead, bear, dead!" the fallen *rulku* said, fighting to aim his thunderstick.

Had the first *rulku* hunter had his senses and sobriety that day, the history of the animal world might have been very different indeed. But the foolish *rulku* didn't. He fidgeted, fighting to aim. *Adyre* attacked, mauling, finishing what his mother bear had started. The *rulku* fought to shoot, but *Adyre* had a fire in him no drunken *rulku* could tame. He bit the hand, the leg. The bear cub then rose, blood dripping from his fangs.

"I said I would kill you," *Adyre* said with a growl. "You aren't worthy to die the same way as my mother. Die slowly–and in pain."

Adyre bit into the neck. Somewhere between that bite and the endless mauling of the paws, the *rulku* was no more. Whatever spirit animal claims the wanton spirit of the man beast finally claimed his. *Adyre* kept mauling until the other bears of the clan approached.

"*Mygrle,*" *Lygra,* or Growl of the Gods, said.

He was a massive grizzly, with reddish brown fur and a river of battle scars nearly the size of the rattlesnakes that jut out from the heart of Bear Mountain. He was *Adyre's* father.

Growl of the Gods turned to see his son, Gentle River, the bear who loved to frolic in streams and watch jumping fish, covered in *rulku* blood.

"The bear gods are with him," an elder bear, *Iyola,* or Wind Whisper, said. "No other cub has faced two *rulku* and survived."

Growl of the Gods contemplated his son, the austere glow of pride and lamentation in his fatherly eyes.

"He is *Adyre* no more," Wind Whisper said. "This day he's earned the name of a warrior. Perhaps *Rulgle,* or *Rulku* Blood."

"No," *Adyre* said. "I will be named after no *rulku*."

"Spoken like a true bear," Growl of the Gods said. "From now on, we will call you *Azaz,* a name that means to be strong, to prevail."

"All hail *Azaz,*" the bears said in a collective growl.

The young cub looked from the body of his mother to the bears before him. Wind Whisper had guessed right. The taste of *rulku* blood was on Azaz's fangs, dripping on his tongue. From that moment, war claimed the heart of the gentle bear as its own.